CW01188956

THE CHRISTMAS CLUE

ALSO BY NICOLA UPSON

The Josephine Tey series
AN EXPERT IN MURDER
ANGEL WITH TWO FACES
TWO FOR SORROW
FEAR IN THE SUNLIGHT
THE DEATH OF LUCY KYTE
LONDON RAIN
NINE LESSONS
SORRY FOR THE DEAD
THE DEAD OF WINTER
DEAR LITTLE CORPSES
SHOT WITH CRIMSON

Other fiction
STANLEY AND ELSIE

NICOLA UPSON
THE CHRISTMAS CLUE

faber

First published in 2025
by Faber & Faber Ltd
The Bindery, 51 Hatton Garden
London EC1N 8HN

Typeset by Faber & Faber Ltd
Printed in the UK by CPI Group (UK) Ltd, Croydon, CR0 4YY

All rights reserved
© Nicola Upson, 2025
Map illustration © Joe McLaren, 2025

The right of Nicola Upson to be identified as author
of this work has been asserted in accordance with Section 77
of the Copyright, Designs and Patents Act 1988

*This is a work of fiction. All of the characters, organizations, and
events portrayed in this novel are either products of the author's
imagination or are used fictitiously*

A CIP record for this book
is available from the British Library

ISBN 978-0-571-39502-6

Printed and bound in the UK on FSC® certified paper in line with our continuing
commitment to ethical business practices, sustainability and the environment.
For further information see faber.co.uk/environmental-policy

Our authorised representative in the EU for product safety is
Easy Access System Europe, Mustamäe tee 50, 10621 Tallinn, Estonia
gpsr.requests@easproject.com

2 4 6 8 10 9 7 5 3 1

In celebration of Anthony and Elva Pratt,
who created *Cluedo*.
And for Veronique Baxter, with love.

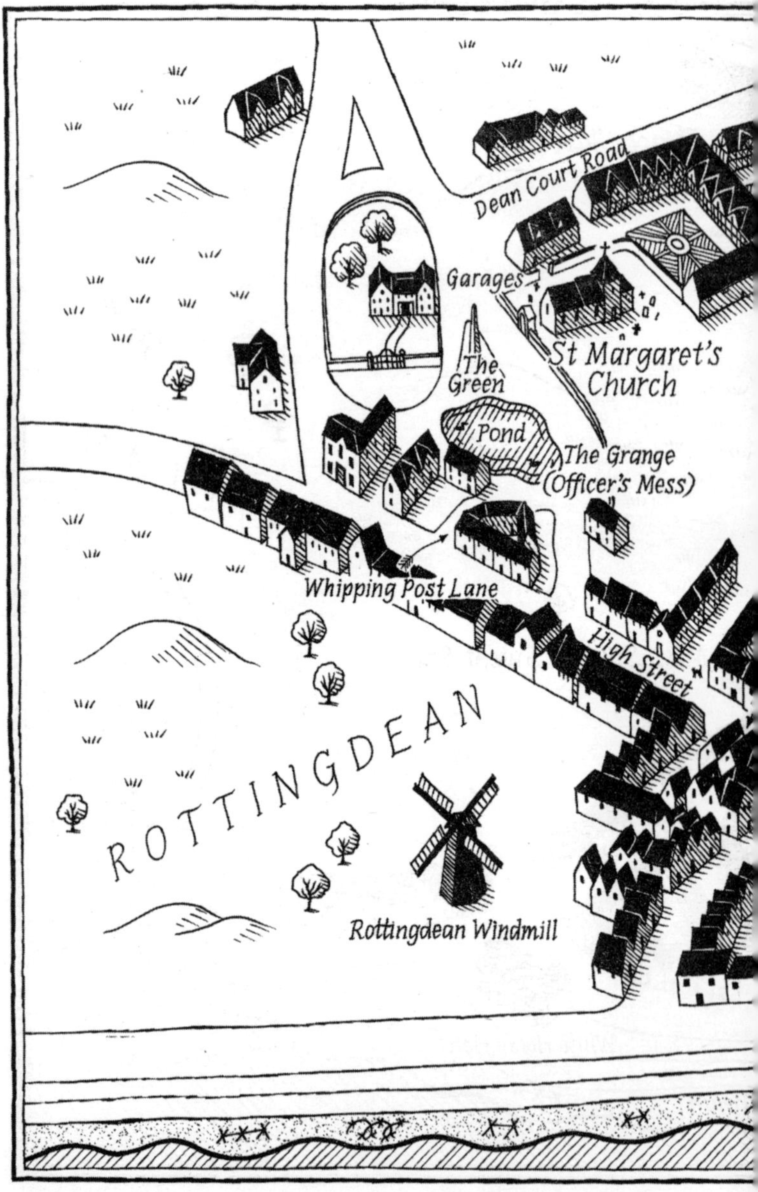
Dean Court Road
Garages
St Margaret's Church
The Green
Pond
The Grange (Officer's Mess)
Whipping Post Lane
High Street
ROTTINGDEAN
Rottingdean Windmill

Tudor Close Hotel

SALTDEAN

Miss Silver's Sweet Shop

White Horse Hotel

Beach

CHRISTMAS 1949

The snow had fallen steadily overnight, bringing its gentle grace to the quiet suburban street. Elva drew back the curtains in the living room and looked out across the garden, as still and timeless as if it were a photograph fixed in a frame. It must be five or six years since Christmas morning had arrived with such picture-book perfection, she thought, then mocked her own vagueness; she knew exactly when the last white Christmas had been, and she would never forget it. Reluctantly, she allowed her eyes to stray to the row of houses a little further down Stanley Road, built to look older than they were, handsome with their beams and tall chimneys. It was unsettling that reminders of Tudor Close – no matter how small – should follow them to their own fireside. There was a time when both she and Anthony had aspired to a house like that, but she was glad now that they had settled for the solid, more dependable semi across the road, free from pretensions and neither more nor less than it claimed to be.

In his excitement at getting home for Christmas Eve, Anthony had forgotten to put the car away in the garage; it stood forlornly in the drive, smothered in white, and Elva knew that it would never start in time to get him to the office on Tuesday. She went to the front door to fetch some logs from the stack in the porch, catching her breath as the cold air hit her face. Next door, the Bulls' children were playing on the lawn, thrilled by the virgin snow, and she could still hear their cries of excitement as she took the logs through to the kitchen to warm by the stove. Anthony was moving about upstairs now, whistling the 'Harry Lime Theme' that had been on his lips since the film came out, so she put the kettle on and took some tea and toast through to the living room, impatient for him to come down and start the day.

Despite her good intentions to do something different with the décor each year, the room invariably settled into the homely, festive feel that both of them preferred. The cards lined up on the piano varied little from year to year – robins chirping hearty greetings, a Dickensian street scene that her cousin had sent them at least twice before – and the tree resisted any attempt to move it to another corner, nestling perfectly between the hearth and the bookcase and dressed with the decorations they had bought for their very first Christmas together. Somehow, the cat had managed to get at the tinsel, even though they'd left the bottom branches bare, and she bent down to tidy it, then straightened the rectangular parcel that sat in pride of place under the tree. She had wrapped it as soon as it arrived, leaving the brown paper on so that the box itself would remain a surprise, and now she had a terrible moment of doubt. What if it wasn't what she thought it was? What if some well-meaning relative had sent them a lavish box of chocolates? Anthony would be so disappointed if the long-awaited parcel turned out to be something different from the one they were expecting.

'Happy Christmas,' he said from the doorway. 'Everywhere looks lovely. *You* look lovely.'

She smiled and gave him a kiss. 'Not bad, is it? I think we've remembered everything.'

'I'm sure we have.' He glanced across the room to the collection of bottles on the sideboard. 'I still think we should have got some port in for your father, though. You know how he likes it.'

'We can't afford it, especially when we don't even drink it ourselves. It'll just sit there going off until next year. Anyway, we've bought him a bottle for Christmas,' she added, nodding to the presents under the tree. 'If he's desperate, he can open that.'

Anthony grinned. 'Shall I lay the table?'

'In a minute. Isn't there something you should do first?'

'Yes, of course. Sorry.'

He moved to pour the tea and Elva laughed in exasperation. 'That's not what I meant!' She picked up the parcel and handed it to him. 'Kids all over the country will be playing their new board game by now, and the man who invented it hasn't even set eyes on the finished product.'

'It wasn't *just* me. We created it together.'

'Then all the more reason why we should open it now, while it's just the two of us. Go on.' Still he hesitated. 'What's the matter?' Elva asked. 'You were awake most of the night, so don't pretend you're not excited.'

'Of course I'm excited, but now it's actually here I've lost my nerve. What if there's something wrong with it? What if people simply don't like it?'

'People will love it, just like we do – just like Waddingtons did from the moment you showed it to them.' She took his face in her hands. 'Anthony Pratt, what do I have to do to make you see how clever you are? It's a brilliant idea, and you've worked so hard to get it right. People will be playing this game for years to come, so stop worrying and enjoy the success. You've earned every bit of it. Now, get that damned box open.'

He did as she ordered, ripping the layers of paper off in a

flourish, and they stared down at the bold black-and-white box. 'Well, you wouldn't miss that in a shop, would you?' Elva said wryly. 'It's wonderful. Very classy.'

Anthony looked at the name splashed flamboyantly across the box, the 'C' dramatically enlarged by a magnifying glass and embellished with a bloody fingerprint. 'I wonder if anyone will really understand why they've called it *Cluedo*? I still think *Murder at Tudor Close* would have been a better title. Not many people play *Ludo* these days.'

'I'm sure they know what they're doing, so we'll just have to trust them. Anyway, after what happened at Tudor Close that year, it might be in poor taste to call it that.'

His face clouded over. 'Yes, of course. I wasn't thinking. When you put it like that, perhaps we shouldn't have done it at all. A board game about murder – people might take against it.'

Elva sighed, wishing she hadn't said anything. Anthony's kindness was one of the things she loved most about him, but sometimes his ability to see all sides of an argument infuriated her. 'Why on earth *shouldn't* we do it? It's just a game, like all those crime novels you read. Have you taken against Agatha Christie?'

'No, of course not.'

'Well then, and she sells thousands of books. Quite

frankly, if people turn against us like that I'll be very happy. Go on – have a look.'

She watched him lift the lid, his eyes bright behind his glasses, an excited child on Christmas morning. He was ten years her senior but it had never felt like that, and suddenly she realised how much she had missed that little boy in their life, the mischievous sense of fun that had brought so much joy to their marriage. He had been a musician before the war, a talented pianist who played for some of the greatest singers and entertained the rich and famous all over the world; his creativity hadn't so much been extinguished by the war as put on hold, sacrificed like so many of the things that ordinary people had given up. He never complained about it, and sometimes Elva wondered if she missed the unpredictability that his music had brought to their lives more than he did, but she longed for him to have something more to look forward to than a desk at the Ministry of Labour. She hadn't said as much to him, reluctant to raise his hopes if the idea didn't take off, but *Cluedo* wasn't just a game to her; it was an investment in their future, a chance to get back the freedom they had loved.

He was unfolding the board now, and she was thrilled to see her own design laid out in front of her, inspired by the room plan of the hotel at Tudor Close. 'This is what makes it, you know,' Anthony said, looking at her with such pride that she felt herself blush. 'It's so bold – exactly what we needed.' He took the miniature weapons out of their bag and started to place them in the various rooms. 'They've done these nicely, too. This piping's made of real lead. Feel the weight of it.'

She picked it up. 'Not bad, but I wish they'd kept the syringe. That was the most sinister thing we came up with, I thought. I always imagined Mrs Peacock carrying it round in her handbag, ready for the right moment.'

'And I had a soft spot for the bomb.'

'Although I suppose that would have made it fairly obvious which room the murder took place in.' She expected Anthony to laugh, but he had begun to glance through the character cards and obviously wasn't listening. He paused, distracted now by one of the colourfully drawn faces, and she didn't need to see the card to know which one it was. 'They've done the whole thing beautifully, though, haven't they?' she said brightly, not wanting this moment to be spoiled for him in any way by memories of the real Tudor Close and the murder that had taken place there. 'And I think they were right to insist on fewer characters than the list we had originally. People would have been playing for hours to get to the solution, and 324 possible permutations is more than enough.' She took the cards from him and shuffled each of the three piles. 'Shall we have a game?'

Anthony looked at the clock. 'Have we got time? What about lunch? You know how your mother hates to eat while the King's on.'

'I did most of the preparations last night, and they won't be here till twelve – probably later now with the snow.' She jumped up and collected the untouched tray. 'You put the murder cards in the envelope while I go and stick the chicken in. I'll bring us a sherry and some mince pies. Let's live dangerously.'

'I'll need more than a sherry if the game doesn't work.'

'Of course it'll work. We spent long enough at this very table making sure it did. I won't be a minute. No peeking at those cards while I'm gone.'

When she returned, the jigsaw that he had spent hours piecing together had been unceremoniously swept back into its box and *Cluedo* now took up the whole table. 'I thought you'd want to be Miss Scarlett,' he said, raising a cheeky eyebrow as he slid the dice over. 'Let's get started.'

They played for an hour, swapping suggestion and counter-suggestion as rooms, characters and murder weapons were steadily eliminated on their respective notepads. Elva watched Anthony relax as the game proved to be everything they had hoped for, his face flushed from excitement and a second sherry. By the time the end was in sight, the solution was obvious to both of them, but the fall of the dice was kinder to Anthony and he reached the crucial room before she had time to make her accusation. 'Colonel Mustard with the dagger in the lounge,' he confirmed triumphantly, taking the cards out of the envelope and laying them face-up on the board. 'Strange, isn't it? That's not how it really happened at all.'

SIX YEARS EARLIER...

1
MISS SILVER, WITH THE WALKING STICK

It seemed to Anthony that the nightshift would never end. There had been no carols or bells to usher in Christmas Eve this year; instead, it had arrived without ceremony to the beating of a hammer on metal and the relentless noise of the drilling machine, until he began to fear for his sanity. He had spent most of the war in this Birmingham munitions factory, making parts for tanks, but the fact that he was used to its horrors didn't make them any better: twelve-hour shifts with no windows and only artificial light, until he lost track of whether it was night or day; the sickly smell of chemicals, which gave him a permanent headache; and the monotony of the work, often on such a minute scale that his eyesight – never good – had deteriorated beyond all repair. But it was the noise he struggled with most – merciless and discordant, everything he hated – and when he shut his eyes to sleep he could still hear it pounding in his head. If someone ever asked him what he dreamed of from an end to the war, it wouldn't be safety or even freedom; it would be silence.

Just when he was beginning to think that the foreman's watch must actually have stopped, the ten o'clock siren sounded to signal the end of the shift and he was a free man, at least for the next three days. One of the supervisors had got hold of some whisky and he eked it out amongst the workers on the factory floor, handing it over with their pay packets. Anthony swigged back his share of the Christmas cheer, glad of something bracing to wake him up, then followed his workmates through to the locker room to change out of his overalls.

'Blimey, Tony, mate – you scrub up well,' Eric said, eyeing the tweed jacket that was well-worn but still smart. 'Anyone would think it was Christmas.'

Anthony grinned, used to the gentle teasing and resigned to the fact that he would always be 'Tony, mate'. It used to grate in the early days, but now he appreciated the camaraderie. 'Elva's picking me up from here and we're going straight to Rottingdean,' he said. 'I won't have a chance to change before we get there.'

'Course, you're off to your posh hotel, aren't you? All right for some. How on earth did you wangle it?'

'Special invitation from the manager. We used to go there a lot before the war – to work, I mean, never as guests. They hired me to play the piano in the evenings, and we'd both help out if they were having special events. Dances or a murder-mystery weekend, that sort of thing.'

'Nice work if you can get it,' Frank said.

'It *was* a good life,' Anthony admitted, half apologetic for having ever had fun when there was very little now to smile about. 'And back then it really was a posh hotel. Lots of famous people stayed there; it was very popular. But I doubt we'll even recognise the place now. Half of it's been requisitioned and the rest is just about to be. This is supposed to be one last hurrah before it all disappears, and we're the entertainment. I hope I haven't lost my touch.' He glanced down at his hands, once his pride and joy but now covered in oil sores and pitted with sharp metal splinters; Elva always joked that she had fallen in love with him for his pianist's fingers. 'It won't be like the old days, though, will it?' he said ruefully. 'Nothing ever is.'

'Still, I bet they'll look after you all right. They'll know people on the black market – those places always do. You won't be sitting down to a sliver of frozen beef like the rest of us.'

'Speak for yourself,' Eric said, feigning indignation. 'My wife's got a recipe for stuffing out of the paper and she swears if I close my eyes I'll think I'm eating turkey.'

'I eat everything my wife cooks with my eyes closed,' Frank scoffed, 'but it still tastes like burnt rubber.'

'Bet you wouldn't say that to her face. If she heard you, I know where the stuffing would go and it wouldn't be on your plate.'

They collected their things and walked out into the street, glad to have some fresh air in their lungs. The leaden sky seemed like a natural continuation of the world inside the factory, neither light nor dark, just a bland, unsympathetic mass of grey. Anthony hoped that the threatening snow would hold off until they got to Sussex.

'I reckon you ought to organise one of them murder-mystery things for round here after Christmas,' Eric called back over his shoulder as they went their separate ways. 'I can think of a few people I'd like to bump off once the season of goodwill's out the way.'

Frank's retort was lost in the sound of a car horn from across the road, urgent and insistent, and Anthony's heart lifted when he saw Elva waiting for him. She jumped out of the Austin and went round to open the passenger door. 'Your carriage awaits,' she said, with a mock chauffeur salute, 'but first I'll have a kiss.'

'My pleasure.'

She drew back and rubbed a smudge of oil from his

forehead. 'I'll drive so you can get some sleep on the way. You must be shattered.'

'I am a bit, but don't you want some help with the map? We haven't got enough petrol to get lost. It'll be touch and go to make it stretch as it is.'

'Oh ye of little faith! I've had a look at the route and it's perfectly straightforward. I'll wake you up if I need you.' Anthony agreed, doubting that he would be able to sleep much anyway while they were travelling but glad of the chance to rest his eyes. 'Anyway, we used to do this two or three times a year before the war,' Elva added, 'so I'm hoping it will all come flooding back to me.'

He climbed into the front seat, hating those three words 'before the war' that seemed to intrude so often on their conversation, coming down like a glass screen to separate them from the life they used to know whilst leaving it tantalisingly within reach. He could only ever say this to Elva, because it seemed wrong when people were losing their lives and their homes, but sometimes he almost welcomed the bombing as a break from the boredom of war. As selfish as it was, he missed the sparkle of those parties with friends or the excitement of boarding a cruise ship, the weekend gatherings at Tudor Close when you never knew who you might bump into on the stairs. Bette Davis, Cary

Grant, Basil Rathbone, Charles Laughton – they had met them all, counted some of them as passing friends, but all that was gone now and he doubted that it would ever come back, at least not in the same way. His feelings weren't as shallow as they sounded, and he was brave enough to acknowledge that what he *really* missed was the person he'd been back then. Surely Elva must wonder sometimes where that Anthony had gone? In his darkest moments, he worried that the more recent version might not prove enough for her.

She reached across to squeeze his hand, putting his fears to rest as she so often did without even realising it. 'I can hardly believe we're doing this,' she said, pulling out into the traffic. 'What a lovely surprise to come out of the blue like that. I can't wait to see the place again, and the village. We can visit all our old haunts, walk by the sea on Christmas morning. Three glorious days to forget about the whole bloody mess.'

Her excitement was infectious, and Anthony vowed there and then to leave his black mood behind with his factory overalls. He looked to the back seat, where his tails were hanging in a clothes bag on a hook by the window, and noticed for the first time how much luggage they had brought. 'What on earth have you packed?' he asked, prodding the two bulging suitcases. 'We're not staying till Easter.'

'Well, obviously I've had to bring your Christmas presents,' she said. 'I noticed just in time that you'd put mine in the car, even though we'd agreed to save the space and have them when we got back. That's a terrible thing to do to a girl. How would I have felt on Christmas morning?'

Anthony looked sheepish. 'Sorry. I just didn't want you to have to wait.'

'Then I've packed every single bit of warm clothing we own. I remember what Tudor Close can be like in the depths of winter, with all those wooden floors and draughty corridors.' She shivered at the thought of it. 'Anyway, I shouldn't be chatting away to you like this. You need to get some rest if you're going to make it to midnight. There are some sandwiches behind the seat if you're hungry.'

He closed his eyes, still doubtful that he would sleep, but they were barely beyond the outskirts of Birmingham when he was ambushed by the warmth and gentle motion of the car. The next thing he knew, Elva was shaking his arm. 'Looks like we're getting a white Christmas after all. Isn't that beautiful?' She had pulled over by the side of the road, and the landscape he awoke to was such a contrast to the city they had left behind that for a moment he thought he was still dreaming. Perched on the crest of a hill, they had the Downs stretched out before them, a patchwork of fields and hedges and villages, rising and falling in perfect harmony, more precious now than ever because somehow they had remained unscathed except for this gentle veiling of snow. 'I knew you'd want me to wake you here,' Elva said. 'It was always the start of the trip for us, do you remember? We'd sit here for ages sometimes.' She spoke as if recalling something that had happened half a lifetime ago, as if they were an elderly couple having one final adventure, and he found something both sad and comforting in the idea. Could it really only be five years since they had made this journey? 'I was frightened that it might all be different now,' she admitted quietly, 'but it's almost as if it's been waiting for us.'

In the distance, a wintry sky weighed heavily on the horizon and large flakes of snow began to flatten themselves against the windscreen, each one disappearing to be replaced by two more as the clouds stepped up their efforts in an eagerness to please. 'We'd better get a move on,' Elva said reluctantly, 'otherwise the roads into the village won't be passable. At least we haven't got far to go.' She winked at Anthony, obviously having the very same thought that had just occurred to him. 'It wouldn't be so bad if we got snowed *in*, though, would it?'

They pressed on, passing through familiar villages in good time and picking up the Rottingdean road just as the light was beginning to fade. 'It's hard to believe that we're almost at the coast,' Elva said, peering through the windscreen at the pretty cottages and village greens that were synonymous with rural England. 'You'd never know that all the drama of the sea was barely a mile away. I think that's what I love most about this place. You get the best of both worlds, so you never tire of either of them.'

'*Murder at the Vicarage* and *Rebecca* all rolled into one,' Anthony said, and laughed as she raised her eyes to the heavens. 'Dean Court Road is the next turning on the left.' She nodded but didn't slow down, and Anthony repeated the direction. 'Well, it *was* the next left,' he said, staring back over his shoulder. 'Now you'll have to go round the pond and come back.'

'I will, but not just yet,' Elva said. 'I've got to pick up your final Christmas present before we check in. Why do you think I've been putting my foot down?'

'Other than that reckless streak I love so much?'

'Other than that, yes.'

'Then I've no idea. What could you possibly be buying from Rottingdean high street this late in the day?'

'Miss Silver's been saving me her best box of cigars. I telephoned her as soon as I knew we were coming, and she very kindly put them by.'

'Cigars? That's extravagant.'

'It is, isn't it?' she said proudly. 'Blame my reckless streak.'

He leant over to kiss her on the cheek. 'Thank you, but will Miss Silver still be open, do you think? If she's got any sense, she'll be settling down for Christmas by her own fireside.'

'She knows we're driving down today, so she said to ring the bell if she's closed. Anytime before six is fine. After that, she doesn't answer the door to anybody, "not even the good Lord himself", apparently. Sorry, that was supposed to be a Sussex accent.'

'Thank God. I felt stupid for never realising that Miss Silver came from Donegal.'

Elva drove slowly down the hill to the centre of the village, past the pond and the entrance to Whipping Post Lane, where a magnificent chestnut tree now stood serenely on the spot once used to punish criminals. 'I'm glad we didn't leave it any later,' she said, nodding to the untouched gardens where the snow was beginning to settle. 'We should just make it back to the hotel before the roads get difficult.'

As soon as they turned onto the high street, they saw the lights from Miss Silver's sweet shop spilling out onto the pavement, a last, defiant bit of seasonal cheer before the impending blackout. A car was parked outside with its engine running, and as they approached a man left the shop and climbed into the passenger seat, clutching a box-shaped parcel. 'I hope they're not my cigars,' Anthony said.

'My money would be on last-minute chocolates for his wife.' Elva pulled into the space that the other car had just vacated, a neat dark rectangle amid the covering of white. 'At least Miss Silver's not staying open just for us.'

The shop was one of a terrace of small cottages, identical to its neighbours except for the colourful array of sweets and novelties in the window and a discreet sign above the door: Miss E. Silver, Tobacconist and Confectioner, est. 1929. 'You could trace my whole childhood in those jars,' Anthony said, looking wistfully at the gobstoppers, humbugs and sugar mice. 'It must be a lovely thing to own a sweet shop, don't you think? You'd only ever have happy customers.'

Elva looked sceptical. 'I think you'd be bored to tears,' she said. 'Three months and you'd never want to look at another barley sugar.'

The bell rang over the door as they entered, and a chill wind blew into the shop with them, sending snowflakes scurrying ahead to the counter. There was no sign of Miss Silver, but a wireless was playing quietly in the background. 'Carols from King's,' Anthony said. 'Now Christmas really has started.' The shop had been splendidly decorated for the season: a tree stood in the corner, dressed with beautiful, old-fashioned glass ornaments that probably came from Miss Silver's own childhood; and a doll's house took up most of the low table by the counter, ready with a box of tiny decorations that customers could amuse themselves in arranging. If he were cynical, Anthony would have said that the magic had been carefully designed to make children linger in the shop and appeal to their parents' weaker nature, but from what he could remember, Ethel Silver was a kind woman, a little childlike herself, and he had no doubt that the efforts were well-meant.

'Look at this,' Elva said, picking up a harlequin mask that was part of the window display. 'It's from the very first Christmas murder mystery we hosted at Tudor Close. Do you remember?'

'Of course. Miss Silver used to love them, didn't she? She was game for anything, too. Always threw herself into any role we gave her. Perhaps she's coming this year.'

'No, she isn't. I asked her when we spoke about the cigars and she said that she couldn't face the Tudor this year. I wanted to ask why, but there was something in her voice that made me feel like I was prying.' She put the mask back in the window. 'I wonder where she is? I thought she'd have heard the bell.'

'There's another one on the counter. Try that.'

Elva did as he suggested. 'Ah, she's got your cigars ready.'

She held up the box, wrapped in tissue and tied with a red ribbon. 'My God, look at the size of it!' Anthony said. 'You've certainly ordered the prize turkey in the poulterer's window.'

Elva laughed. 'The one as big as you? She's gone to such trouble. It's very kind of her.'

'I still don't think you should have been so extravagant.'

'Well, your mum chipped in, too, and I wanted you to have something special.' She took his hand and spoke more seriously. 'You work so hard in that damned factory and I know you hate it, but you never complain. We said we'd make this trip as much like the old days as we could, so what's the harm in a bit of luxury that we wouldn't normally allow ourselves? They're the same brand as that cigar Errol Flynn gave you when he was here. You were so thrilled you didn't smoke it for months.'

'And then I wished I hadn't. I should have put it in a glass case, preserved it for posterity.'

'Bugger posterity. What's the point, especially these days?' She opened her handbag and rummaged inside for her coupons. 'She'll be in trouble if she doesn't get that window covered soon. I don't think there's an ARP warden alive who knows what Christmas spirit is. Do you think she's popped out for something?'

'And left the shop open? I doubt it. Anyway, she must have been here to serve that man we saw leaving.' Anthony rang the bell again, less politely this time; when there was still no sign of the shopkeeper, he went over to the door that led to her private quarters. 'Miss Silver? Are you there? It's Anthony and Elva.'

'I hope she's all right,' Elva said, and there was an uneasiness in her voice that was beginning to trouble him, too.

'I'm sure she is, but I'll go and look for her. You wait here in case she *has* gone out. We don't want her to come back and find us lurking in her house. We'll give the poor woman a heart attack.'

A short corridor led off the shop, running between a storeroom piled with boxes and the doorway to a narrow staircase, covered by a curtain. The storeroom was in darkness, so Anthony went through to a small but comfortable kitchen-parlour which was obviously where Miss Silver spent most of her time: there was a pleasantly cluttered, lived-in feel to the room, but its only occupant at present was a magnificent male tabby cat, stretched out on a blanket by the warmth of the stove. The cat lifted its head and yawned as Anthony entered the room, and he bent down to stroke it. 'Where's your mistress, Tabs?' he asked, but the cat seemed oblivious to any urgency in the question and got up to finish a dish of offal that stood by the back door. For a moment, Anthony wondered if Miss Silver had gone outside and slipped on the snow, then he saw that the door was locked and firmly bolted; no one had left the house that way.

He turned back to try upstairs, automatically pushing the storeroom door open wider as he passed, and something caught his eye, a dim, shadowy outline that felt out of place. When he flicked the light switch on, the sight that greeted him was faintly comedic and it took him a second or two to register the thin, stockinged legs sticking out from between piles of boxes, like the Wicked Witch of the East. Then something in their stillness brought him to his senses and he ventured further into the room. Miss Silver was lying face down on the floor, a circle of blood spilling out from beneath her head in a parody of a halo, sticky and viscous and bright, and looking bizarrely like red paint in the artificial glare of the electric light. A walking stick had been abandoned next to her, its handle covered with blood, and Anthony had no doubt that it had been used to beat her. His legs threatened to go from under him and he grabbed at the door to steady himself, switching off the light in an attempt to block out the horror while he waited for the nausea to pass.

He must have cried out in shock, because he heard Elva's voice from the shop, followed by the click of her heels on the tiled floor. 'Anthony, what's happened? Have you found her?' Hurriedly, he closed the door and barred her way into the room, but there was no hiding his stricken face. 'My God, Anthony, what on earth's wrong?'

'Miss Silver's in there,' he said, struggling to contain the panic he felt welling up inside him. 'It looks like someone's beaten her to death.' He saw the shock in his wife's eyes, quickly replaced by horror, and wished he had chosen his words more carefully. 'There's nothing we can do except call the police.'

Elva stared at him in disbelief, then tried to push past him. 'There must be *something* . . .'

'Darling, no. It's too late.'

'Are you *sure* she's dead?'

The image flashed again in his head, merciless in its

clarity. 'Yes, I'm sure.' He put his arm around his wife and led her through to the parlour. 'Trust me, she's beyond our help. We need to get the experts in.'

'Do you think it was the man we saw leaving who did it?' Elva asked, and Anthony hated the fear in her eyes; desperately, he wished that he felt braver. 'It must have been, mustn't it? There wasn't time for it to be anyone else.'

'I don't know,' he said doubtfully. 'He might have been a perfectly ordinary customer, waiting for her like we were. Perhaps he just gave up and left. This could have happened long before any of us got here.'

'But he had a parcel, Anthony. She must have served him. If we'd been a few minutes earlier, we might have been able to save her.'

Or we might have taken a knock over the head for our trouble, Anthony thought, but didn't say as much. 'Does she have a telephone?' he asked instead. 'You said you spoke to her.'

'Yes, it's in the shop. I saw it by the counter.'

'Right, let's go and report what's happened.'

But before they could do anything, they heard the tinkle of the bell above the door as someone opened and closed it. 'My God, what if they've come back?' Elva whispered in a panic.

'Why would they risk that? Whoever did this will be miles away by now.'

'Perhaps they left something behind, something incriminating.'

'It's much more likely to be another customer or the ARP,' he said rationally, but the alarm in his voice belied any attempt to be reassuring. 'I'll go and see.'

Before she could stop him, he pushed through to the shop, coming face to face with two men in dark overcoats. It was hard to say who was more surprised, but the elder of the two strangers recovered himself first. 'Detective Inspector Clough,' he said, fishing a warrant card out of his inside pocket. 'And this is Detective Sergeant Devonshire. Might I ask who you are, sir?'

'Inspector, thank God you're here,' Anthony said, unable to hide his relief. 'I was just about to telephone you.'

'Really, sir?' Clough said, exchanging a sceptical glance with his colleague. 'And why might that be?'

'It's Miss Silver, the lady who runs the shop. She's been murdered. My wife and I called in to collect some cigars, and I found her . . .' He tailed off as Elva joined him, suddenly aware of how suspicious he sounded. 'Why are *you* here?' he asked. 'How did you know that something had happened?'

'We've had reports of a disturbance, sir,' the sergeant said. 'The woman next door heard raised voices and what she thought was a scream, so she called us straight away. People try their luck at Christmas and she was worried that it might be a burglary, so we got here as soon as we could.'

'It's a pity it wasn't sooner,' Elva retorted with feeling. 'You might have been able to save her.'

Anthony loved his wife's spirit but questioned the wisdom of antagonising the police when their own position was so delicate; they had no way of proving how long they had been at the shop or what they had done while they were there, and the truth sounded a little fanciful even to his own ears. His fears proved justified. 'Whereas you were right on hand, madam,' the inspector said sarcastically. 'We'll have some questions for you and your husband in a minute, but first we'll need to look at the body. Where is it?' Anthony went to show them, flinching at the impersonal request, but the sergeant blocked his way. 'Just tell us please, sir,' he said. 'We don't want you contaminating the scene.'

The words 'any more than you have already' hung unspoken in the air. 'She's in the storeroom,' Anthony said. 'It's just through there on the left, before you get to the parlour.'

'Thank you, sir.' He pulled down the blackout blind and slipped the catch up on the door. 'Now, if you'll go and wait in the back, we'll be with you as soon as we can. And don't touch anything.'

Anthony and Elva went meekly through to the parlour and perched on the edge of the two fireside chairs. The shock was receding now, replaced by a sadness that only intensified as Anthony looked round the room. It seemed wrong that they should be sitting here in Miss Silver's lounge, staring at her things when she would never use them again, and he could see that Elva felt as uncomfortable about it as he did. After the trouble Miss Silver had taken to make the shop look so beautiful for the time of year, the lack of Christmas in this room was striking. It was almost as if she had known that there was no point in making the effort, that she wouldn't be here to appreciate it.

'What a bloody mess we're in,' Elva said with a sigh. 'They think we've got something to do with it, don't they? I'm so sorry. I wish I'd never brought us here. We could be sitting in the bar with a gin and tonic by now.'

'You were only trying to do something nice. We'll just stay calm and tell them exactly what happened. They'll *have* to believe us.'

The detectives were only gone a minute or two, and their return made the room seem cramped and claustrophobic. 'Right then, let's start with some names,' Clough said, making no reference to the horror or sadness of what he had just seen.

It must take a certain kind of temperament to be a policeman, Anthony thought, suddenly missing the compassion that he loved so much in detective novels. 'I'm Anthony Pratt and this is my wife, Elva.'

'You're not from round here, are you?'

'No, we're staying at Tudor Close for Christmas. It's work,' he added, seeing the expression of resentment cross the sergeant's face. 'We haven't just come to enjoy ourselves.'

'And what work might that be?'

'I'm a pianist,' Anthony said, deciding that it wasn't the moment to mention murder mysteries. 'I provide all the music for the weekend.'

'You knew the victim, though? You used her name when we got here.'

Anthony was tempted to point out that it was above the door for all to see, but there was no point in arguing when Clough was right. 'Yes, we've known her for ten years or so.'

'Not very well,' Elva clarified, 'but we've been coming to the Tudor since the early days. Miss Silver was often there, and we shop here whenever we come. We exchanged Christmas cards, but we didn't know her well enough to have a reason to kill her.' She collected herself, seeing the frown cross the inspector's face, and spoke with more restraint. 'As I said, we were only here to collect some cigars. They're on the counter.'

'Tell us what happened when you got here, sir.' Anthony did as he was asked, beginning with the car they had seen outside. 'And what can you tell us about these people?'

'Not much, I'm afraid. The man was wearing a hat and scarf, so I've no idea what he looked like. The car was a dark colour – black or grey, but it was hard to tell which in the dusk.'

'I suppose a number plate would be too much to hope for?' Anthony nodded. 'What about the driver?'

'A woman, I think,' Elva said cautiously. 'It looked to me as if she was wearing a red hat, but it might have been a headscarf. She was hunched down in the seat, so it's hard to tell. To be honest, we were both paying more attention to the shop. It looked so beautiful in the snow. The perfect image of Christmas.'

'Thinking about it, though, they must have been parked

here for a while,' Anthony added. 'There was no snow under their car when they drove off, you see. Everywhere else had a good covering by then.'

'Very useful, sir. Anything else?' They both shook their heads. 'Well, we know where you are if we need you. We'd better have your home address, too,' he added, 'just in case you decide to leave early.'

'It's 9 Stanley Road, King's Heath, Birmingham. Can we go now?'

'Yes, you can. Don't forget your cigars.'

'But we haven't paid for them.'

'I wouldn't worry about that, madam,' Clough said in a kindlier tone. 'Miss Silver's hardly likely to mind, is she? Happy Christmas.'

They walked sadly out into the street and Anthony put the cigars on the back seat. 'Are all policemen so brutal in real life, do you think, or was it just them?'

'Mercifully I haven't met enough to say. Will you drive now? I don't fancy that hill.'

He nodded absentmindedly, then suddenly realised what had been nagging at him. 'Margery Wren!' he said. 'Of course.'

'Who?'

'Margery Wren. That's what this reminds me of. She was

murdered in her own sweet shop in Ramsgate – 1930, I think it was, beaten round the head just like Miss Silver.' Elva sighed and shook her head, obviously not in the mood for her husband's encyclopaedic knowledge of true crime, which tested her patience at the best of times. Wherever they were, he could invariably conjure up a tale of murder and mayhem until their holidays threatened to become a guided tour of the crime scenes of England. 'There was a woman in a red hat there, too,' he added, hoping that might pique her interest.

'And was she the murderer?'

Anthony shrugged. 'No one knows. The crime was never solved.'

'You're surely not suggesting that there's a killer on the loose, targeting middle-aged spinsters who sell confectionery?'

'Well, Ramsgate's not *that* far away.' He smiled. 'Of course not, but Miss Wren's is an interesting case. She survived the initial attack for a few days, and they think she knew her killer, but she wouldn't say who it was.'

'At least Miss Silver didn't suffer like that. I hope it was quick.'

'Yes, so do I.' Anthony shivered, thinking about how frightened the shopkeeper must have been. It was a relief to be off the premises, and he was glad when the engine started on the second attempt. 'And you needn't worry,' he said, turning the car round in the road. 'I've gone right off that sweet shop idea.'

2
IN THE BEDROOM, WITH AN IDEA

It was only a short drive to Tudor Close, but the snow was coming down in a silent, purposeful storm now, and they could have travelled ten fair-weather miles in the time it took them to reach their destination. Anthony drew the car up alongside the hotel's elegant but unassuming roadside entrance, a pair of heavy oak doors studded with ironwork and firmly shut against the evening.

'Not the warmest of welcomes,' Elva said wryly, 'and the blackout doesn't help.' The lack of light from inside gave the sprawling building a cold, forbidding look, amplified by its isolated position at the edge of the village. As she got out of the car, she could sense rather than see the lonely downland that stretched before them; curiously, its openness was oppressive, a landscape of absences – sound, movement, light – that managed to be both magical and threatening. She shivered, feeling exposed and vulnerable after the shock of the afternoon, and had a sudden pang to be back at home in Stanley Road, where everything was safe and familiar.

Anthony seemed to share her unease, and his earlier

enthusiasm for the trip had all but disappeared. 'Do you think anyone will have the heart for a murder-mystery game once word gets out that there's been a real murder in the village?' he asked doubtfully.

'The staff will be local, but I doubt that any of the guests will have known Miss Silver,' Elva said, invariably more cynical than her husband. 'It's just a headline to them, a scandal they can speculate about over dinner. If anything, it might add an extra frisson to the occasion. The hotel will probably start wishing it had charged more for the tickets.'

'I hadn't thought of that.'

'You're far too trusting.'

As she crossed the threshold, Elva found it easy to imagine herself back in a different time, even though she knew that the building's authenticity was an illusion: Tudor it might be in name and appearance, but it had been built in the 1920s, converted from a farmhouse and various outbuildings into luxurious terraced houses standing on three sides of a quadrangle. Rottingdean had been luckier than other parts of the country, where bland modern dwellings had sprung up to counteract a desperate shortage of homes after the last war, altering picturesque villages beyond all recognition. But the men who saw a commercial value in Rottingdean's old-world charm had been out of touch with what people were willing or able to pay, no matter how close to Brighton or accessible to London the village was, and only one of the seven houses built had ever been sold. Tudor Close's later success as a resort of choice for the rich and famous had allowed the failure to be conveniently forgotten, the accepted story being that the design was arousing so much interest that its owners abandoned the houses for a hotel that more people could enjoy. But Elva had often wondered what it must have been like for that single family to rattle around in it alone in the early years, having the strange beauty of the place to themselves; she had never been able to decide if it would have delighted her or driven her slowly mad.

Two of the self-contained houses remained as suites for larger parties or guests who wanted more privacy, and the rest of the hotel was arranged in conventional style – a variety of public rooms, all furnished with period decorations to match the Tudor exterior. In the entrance hall, a sorry-looking Christmas tree seemed to pre-date the hotel's existence, but it certainly wasn't the heat of the room that had caused the needles to drop in such profusion. A half-hearted fire had been left to burn so low in the grate that there seemed little chance of reviving it, even if someone had been inclined to try, and when Elva put her hand surreptitiously on the radiator, it was stone cold. The war years had obviously taken their toll on the hotel's fortunes and she caught Anthony's eye, sharing a look of disappointment. Christmas had been magical here in the old days, but it was hard to believe that anything in this room had ever sparkled.

At the reception desk, a silver-haired man in his late fifties was doing his best to placate an angry couple, and she recognised him as the manager, Reginald Browning, whom they had met on previous visits. In truth, only half the couple was angry; the woman stood at a distance from her husband, not so much embarrassed by his show of temper as weary of it. 'I want the set of rooms I booked, damn it,' he was saying, 'and booked weeks ago, I might add. My wife and I are depending on it. It's the only reason we're here.'

'I'm very sorry about the mix-up, Professor Rivers,' Browning said, and Elva admired the polite but non-committal tone in his voice. 'I'm not sure how it can have happened.'

'I don't care how it happened, just get it sorted. My nurse is travelling with us, and apart from anything else we need the space.'

'I do understand, and the suite I've reserved for you is

the mirror image of the other one, so there'll be plenty of space for Nurse Blanchett. And if anything, the master bedroom is a little bigger.'

'But they're not the rooms I booked, are they?' He paused and closed his eyes, rubbing his forehead as if trying to stave off a migraine. His hand was trembling, Elva noticed, and she realised that his temper made him appear stronger than he was. 'Move the other woman into the suite you're trying to give us,' he continued, 'and honour the arrangement we made with you. That's all I'm asking.'

'I'm afraid that's not possible, sir. Mrs Threadgold arrived a few days ago and she's very settled in number seven now. She's asked not to be disturbed, and I wouldn't want to inconvenience her.'

'But you're happy to inconvenience me? Christ, Browning, I'd forgotten how infuriating you can be. You know why we want our old rooms. It's the last chance we'll get to see our home as it was before the army moves in and does God knows what to it.' Elva glanced at Anthony, intrigued by the faintly personal turn that the exchange had taken. 'You're enjoying this, aren't you?' Rivers continued. 'I wouldn't be surprised if you'd done it deliberately to spite me. Is that what this is all about? Paying me back because you were unhappy when you worked for me all those years ago? I should have realised. No one can hold a grudge quite like a servant.'

If Browning was offended by the outburst, he didn't show it. 'I can assure you that's not the case, sir,' he said evenly. 'It was a long time ago, and it brought me to the Tudor. I've been very happy here.'

'We'll see about that. Where's the owner? I want to speak to him.'

'Impossible, I'm afraid. His son's home on leave and he's spending Christmas with his family. I've had orders not to disturb him on any account.'

'This really is outrageous. I've a good mind to go somewhere else.'

It was a vain expression of defiance in this weather, and Elva thought she detected a twinkle in Browning's eye as he called his guest's bluff. 'You're welcome to try the White Horse Hotel,' he said, looking pointedly towards the window, where snow was accumulating steadily against the leaded glass. 'We'd be sorry to lose you, of course, but I could put a call in for you now and see if they have a vacancy at this late stage?'

Rivers obviously knew when he was beaten. 'Very well. We'll take number one, but I expect the inconvenience to be reflected in my bill.'

'Of course, sir.' Browning selected a key from the cupboard behind the desk and began to ask about luggage, but Rivers snatched the key and turned away. He walked across the hall to the lift, and Elva noticed how tightly he was gripping his wife's hand.

Anthony raised a conspiratorial eyebrow, but Browning greeted them as if nothing had happened. 'Mr and Mrs Pratt, how lovely to see you again. Welcome back to the Tudor, and a very happy Christmas to you both.'

'And the same to you. We don't usually find you on reception, though.'

'You do these days, sir. On reception, in the restaurant, and as like as not behind the bar.'

'Gosh.'

'Well, we're all having to get used to doing more than we used to. Staff duties aren't quite as clear-cut as they were the last time you were here, I'm sorry to say.'

'So you don't need the guests making things even more difficult for you,' Elva said sympathetically, still intrigued by the exchange they had just overheard. 'That couple – the Riverses – are they the people who lived here before it was a hotel? And you worked for them?'

'That's right, Mrs Pratt. I was their butler-cum-chauffeur. A few of us here were on the staff, but it was a long time ago now. A very long time.' He turned the page on the register in front of him, apparently drawing a line under the subject. 'Anyway, how are you both?'

'A bit shaken, to be honest,' Anthony said. 'We had a terrible shock on our way here.'

'I'm sorry to hear that. What happened?'

Elva hesitated, but the police hadn't asked them not to tell anyone. 'It's Miss Silver,' she said. 'We popped into the village to collect some cigars and found her . . .'

She tailed off, leaving Anthony to complete the sentence. 'We found her in the storeroom of her shop,' he said, lowering his voice. 'I'm afraid she's dead.'

Browning reeled as though he were going to fall, but held on to the desk for support. 'Miss Silver? But she can't be. I was in the shop myself earlier this afternoon and she was perfectly all right – looking forward to Christmas, in fact, and in very good spirits.' He shook his head in disbelief. 'She didn't seem ill, not in the slightest. What was it? Her heart?'

'No, nothing like that. Someone had assaulted her. The police think it was a burglary.'

That wasn't strictly true, Elva thought; the police had said very little, and, as far as she was aware, they hadn't even checked the till to see if the takings were missing.

'Could I ask you to keep this to yourselves, just for now?' Browning asked.

'Yes, of course. Not quite what the guests are expecting, I don't suppose. A little too close for comfort.'

'Oh it's not that, Mr Pratt. No, it's Miss Silver's sister, Mrs Grayson. She's the cook here, you see. I'll have to go and break the news to her, but I wouldn't want her to overhear any tittle-tattle amongst the guests. You know what people are like when they get wind of a tragedy. They make up what they don't know, and the more scandalous the better.'

'Yes, of course,' Anthony said. 'We won't breathe a word, I promise.'

'And please give Mrs Grayson our condolences,' Elva added.

'Thank you. I'll do that. I dare say the police will be here themselves soon enough. Mrs Grayson is Ethel's closest relative, as far as I know. They'll want to talk to her.' He looked up quickly, obviously concerned that his words might be misconstrued. 'Only to let her know what's happening, I mean. Not because they think . . .' The rest of the sentence petered out as Browning pulled himself together. 'Anyway, let's get you checked in.' He ran his finger down the book in front of him. 'Ah yes, you're in number six, above the dining room. We thought that would be most convenient. Here are the keys – one for the room and one for the garage.'

'Lovely, thank you.'

Elva took the keys while Anthony signed the register. 'When would be the best time for us to talk to the actors?' he asked. 'Have they arrived yet or are they coming first thing in the morning?'

Browning looked puzzled. 'The actors?'

'That's right – the actors you've booked for the murder mystery. We'll need to explain the story to them and flesh out their characters ready for the afternoon entertainment.' He touched the side of his nose. 'Let them know whodunit, throw in a few red herrings, that sort of thing.'

'I'm very sorry, Mr Pratt,' Browning said, obviously embarrassed, 'but there are no actors.'

'No actors?'

'No, sir, not this year. The war's put paid to that. Everyone who used to be involved is either away on duty or picking up the slack at home. We rather hoped that you and Mrs Pratt would have devised something to fit the current situation. Perhaps we should have been more specific in our invitation, but we just assumed, with things the way they are, that you'd realise . . .'

'Of course, Mr Browning, we should have checked,' Elva

said hurriedly, before the situation got any more awkward. 'It's really not a problem.'

'But . . .' Anthony started to object.

'We'll think of something, I'm sure.'

'I don't doubt it, Mrs Pratt. You always do. Some of those mysteries you came up with in the old days – well, inspirational, they were. That one based on the old smuggling stories was a classic – and the theatre mystery, where the answer was in the play all along and yet none of us guessed it. I think the staff enjoyed themselves as much as the guests.'

'Then perhaps some of them might like to take part this time?' Anthony suggested hopefully. 'If you could . . .'

Elva jumped in quickly. 'Remember what's happened in the village, darling. Poor Mrs Grayson . . . And anyway, Mr Browning's just told us how busy everyone is.'

'I can ask, though,' Browning said, obviously keen to offer something. 'Someone might be able to help out, other duties permitting.'

Anthony was staring ruefully at a poster behind the desk that advertised the hotel's festive entertainment. It had their names in big letters, promising to brighten everyone's Christmas with a dazzling murder-mystery event, and Elva knew how important it was to him to live up to the billing. 'We'll think of something,' she repeated, as though she could will it to be true.

'We're very grateful, and I'm sure the guests will appreciate your efforts. I've been telling everyone about it as they arrive and they're all looking forward to it. It's the bit of cheer we need at the moment, and who doesn't love a puzzle?' Browning perked up as he turned to Anthony, a more positive note in his voice. 'And there's the piano in the dining room, of course, sir. You're welcome to try that out whenever you like and make sure it's up to scratch.'

Quite what they would do if it wasn't was another matter, but Browning looked like a man who'd been dealt enough problems for one day and Anthony had the tact not to ask. 'Thank you,' he said. 'I'll go down when we've settled in. Is the Bechstein still in the ballroom?'

'Ah yes, but we won't be using the ballroom. It's a shame, but we've had to close some of the rooms. There's no call for them at the moment, and we're watching the costs where we can. On that subject, are you all right to take your own luggage upstairs? There's no bellboy these days – poor Johnny, signed up straight away and went down with the plane on his last training flight. He was only seventeen. I'm happy to give you a hand, but my back . . .'

He gave a theatrical wince which would have passed the

audition for any Christmas entertainment. 'We'll manage,' Anthony said. 'I'm sure you're needed here or with Mrs Grayson.'

Defeated, they went back out to the car. The hotel sign was swinging forlornly in a strengthening wind, and its promise of 'every modern comfort' and 'dancing nightly' suddenly seemed like a very poor joke. 'What a bloody disaster,' Anthony said, his head in his hands. 'All that work we did on the scenario for *Murder at Tudor Close* and we've got no one to perform it.'

'We could double up on some of the roles,' Elva suggested, with more conviction than she felt. 'Perhaps drop a couple of the minor characters.'

'But we need at least six people to make it work. That's the cleverness of the plot. If you and I are going to start coming in and out of doors in wigs and funny accents, we might as well leave now.'

'Oh, I don't know. It worked for that group we went to see in Coventry. Wigs and funny accents were all they had. It was so awful that it was actually entertaining.'

'That wasn't quite the epitaph I was hoping for,' Anthony said. 'Most of these things *are* awful, but we've got standards to maintain. We have a reputation for classy, ingenious whodunits – well, we did before the world went to hell in a handcart.' He opened the passenger door so that she could get in out of the cold. 'Anyway, we didn't bring any wigs.'

Elva couldn't help but imagine Miss Silver's body, lying alone in a darkened storeroom or pored over as an exhibit by the police. There was something faintly indecent about the fact that she and Anthony were at a posh hotel on Christmas Eve, worrying about the quality of an imaginary murder, but she cared more about him than she did about decency and she could see how disappointed he was. 'Let's put the car in the garage, get our luggage inside and go to our room to think,' she suggested. 'I'll ask Browning to rustle up some tea for us.'

'I'm sure they could have found enough people if they'd tried,' Anthony said, struggling to keep control of the car as he reversed into the small yard off the main road that held a row of garages. 'They probably just didn't want to pay them. Times are obviously hard, even at Tudor Close.'

The same thought had occurred to Elva, but there was no point in dwelling on it. 'Come on, Anthony. We've been in tougher scrapes than this one, and finding solutions to impossible situations is what you do best. We'll be laughing about this soon, and it's not as if . . .' She was about to say that it wasn't as if anyone had died, but caught herself just in time. 'It's not as if we're having to pay to be here. At the very least, we'll have a good Christmas.'

They found the garage that corresponded with their room number and Anthony got out to force the double doors back wide enough for Elva to manoeuvre the car inside. 'Thank God for that,' she said, laughing to see how quickly their hats and coats had been covered in snow-flakes. 'Now we're here and ready to settle in, this is actually quite romantic.'

Anthony grinned and brushed the snow off the bonnet of the car, then covered it in rugs against the cold. 'Let's just take the basics inside for now,' he suggested. 'I'll come back for the rest when the snow stops.'

He lifted one of the suitcases out while Elva unhooked the clothes bag and grabbed the ill-fated box of cigars. 'Might as well take any treats we've got,' she said. 'I'm not sure we'll find much luxury inside.'

Despite the cold and wet underfoot, Elva stopped in her tracks as Anthony opened the narrow wooden gate that led through to the hotel's courtyard. Under a full moon, the silhouette of the building was breathtakingly beautiful, its tall chimneys and silvered gables far more dramatic than if they had arrived in daylight. 'Just look at it,' she said, almost in a whisper, 'all secretive and mysterious in the blackout. It might have been designed for a country-house murder.'

Anthony agreed, obviously as inspired as she was. 'Even down to the name. I always think there's something furtive about a close – perfectly normal on the outside, but all sorts of skulduggery going on behind closed doors. If we can't pull something out of the bag here, we ought to be ashamed of ourselves.'

They followed the path round to the hotel's courtyard entrance; or rather, they followed what they *hoped* was the path; no attempt had been made to clear the snow away – another casualty, no doubt, of the staff shortages – and they were glad of the moonlight to guide them. The gardens used to be immaculate, Elva recalled: red-brick pavements artfully overgrown with trailing flowers, borders filled with water features and beautiful statuary. She doubted that she'd find such perfection here now, even in summer, but at least the snow masked any telltale signs of neglect.

The sound of laughter and shouting broke suddenly into the quiet courtyard. It was a rowdiness that Elva would never normally have associated with Tudor Close, but she found it welcome in the unexpectedly subdued atmosphere of the hotel. They stood aside to let the small group of soldiers pass, wishing them a merry Christmas as they went, and she noticed an American accent in the replies. 'That should liven things up a bit,' Anthony said. 'The guest list so far hasn't been very promising.'

They met Browning at the entrance porch, closing the door that the soldiers had left wide open. 'I'm sorry about that,' he said. 'They're not supposed to use the hotel as a shortcut, but there's nothing I can do to stop them.'

'Well, they're a long way from home,' Anthony said cheerfully, 'and we waited ages for America to join the war, so I don't suppose we should grudge them a bit of fun at Christmas.'

The manager's frown suggested otherwise. 'They're Canadian, sir. Princess Patricia's Light Infantry, to be precise. They've been with us for a couple of years now.'

'That's told you,' Elva said, suppressing a smile as they headed for the stairs, 'but a few uniforms around the place *will* be nice. I don't much mind where they're from.' She ran a finger along the banister and looked reproachfully at the dust. 'And I won't worry about my own housekeeping when we get back this time.'

The corridors on the first floor had low ceilings and uneven floors that creaked at the first hint of a footstep. 'Isn't number seven where Bette Davis used to stay?' Anthony said.

'Bette Davis and her entourage, yes. It's one of the original houses and the best suite they have. Four bedrooms and very luxurious – I took a peek once when the staff were cleaning it out. Perhaps this Mrs Threadgold's a film fan, and that's why she doesn't want to move.' They stopped by their own room and Elva looked thoughtfully towards the end of the corridor, where a forbidding oak door marked the upstairs entrance to the suite that everyone seemed to want. 'Why on earth would you come away to a hotel at Christmas if you didn't want to be disturbed?' she asked, speculating about its occupant.

Anthony shrugged. 'It does seem a bit peculiar, but what doesn't at the moment? Perhaps she can't stand her family. The thought of one more Christmas with old Uncle Harry dropping his walnut shells over the best rug was just too much for her. We should probably rule her out of the party games, though.'

Their own room was more welcoming than either of them had dared to hope after the sparseness of the entrance hall. A fire had recently been lit in the grate and the tightly drawn curtains kept the heat in, bringing the first true prospect of warmth that they had felt since arriving in Rottingdean. It was a spacious room, overlooking the courtyard on one side and the sprawling churchyard of St Margaret's on the other, and had been simply furnished in the Tudor style with a large four-poster bed, two comfortable armchairs and a desk by the south-facing window. The décor had some lovely individual touches: a carved over-mantel depicted rural scenes of farmers bringing home the harvest, appropriate to the building's origins, and the graceful Tudor rose that could be seen everywhere around the hotel adorned each corner of their bed. Fir cones and sprigs of holly added to the traditional, rustic charm, and a small anteroom offered discreet hanging space for their clothes; in the far corner, a heavy oak door hid the best surprise of all.

'My God, Anthony, we've got our own bathroom!' Elva squealed in delight. 'No more creeping down those corridors with a sponge bag in the middle of the night. We've never had a room as nice as this before.'

There was a telephone on the desk and she sat down to order some tea while Anthony nurtured the fire. She had to try three times before Browning answered, and assumed that he was breaking the bad news to Mrs Grayson. 'You're sure it's not too much trouble?' she said, when he finally picked up. 'All right, that's lovely – thank you. Would she? Yes, of course. I'll come down in about ten minutes.' She replaced the receiver. 'Mrs Grayson wants to talk about what happened to her sister. It's obviously come as a terrible shock to her, poor woman.'

'Do you want me to come with you?' Anthony offered.

'No, I'll go. There's not really much that I can tell her, and it's probably better that way. She doesn't need to know what you saw, but I can at least be sympathetic.' She handed him a notepad and pencil from the bedside table. 'And you'd better stay here and get thinking. We can't start Christmas until we've worked something out.'

She went down by a different staircase, taking the opportunity to reacquaint herself with the hotel's layout and visit some of the rooms she had always loved. The red lounge and tearoom, the cocktail bar and the cosy central lounge that everyone called the great log room were all still in use, she was pleased to see; only the ballroom and another sitting room seemed to be out of bounds, their doors firmly closed and locked. She walked through the conservatory, feeling sorry for the wall of plants that had no choice but to brave the icy draughts, and found herself back in the old hall. Browning was busy with some guests she hadn't seen before, so she hovered at a polite distance and waited her turn. There was yet another small lounge off the hallway, known as the ladies' writing room, although Elva had never known it to be used exclusively by women or even for that purpose. The room was dimly lit by a single lamp, and from the doorway she could see Mrs Rivers standing by the French windows with the drapes drawn back, looking out into the courtyard. As she watched, the woman put her hand to the glass and for a moment Elva thought she was going to push open the door and walk out into the snow, but she obviously thought better of it and turned back into the room. She jumped when she realised that she wasn't alone and Elva smiled apologetically, noticing that the woman's face was even paler in the shadows, her presence scarcely more tangible than a ghost's. 'I'm sorry, I didn't mean to startle you,' she said. 'We haven't been properly introduced. I'm Elva Pratt and I'm here with my husband, Anthony. We were waiting to check in while you were at reception earlier.'

The woman gave a faint smile, but there was no warmth in it. 'Yes, I remember. Not our finest hour, I'm afraid.' Her voice was low and unemotional, and Elva was reminded of a radio announcer on the brink of delivering bad news. 'I'm Celia Rivers. Please accept my apologies for any unpleasantness.'

'There's really no need. It's always disappointing when plans have to be changed, especially when you've been looking forward to something. Everything seems to matter more at Christmas, doesn't it?'

Mrs Rivers nodded. 'That's certainly true, but I don't think my husband's rudeness can be excused by the season. It seems to flourish perfectly well all year round.' Her candour in front of a stranger was so far removed from conventional English behaviour that it threw Elva for a moment. 'If you'll excuse me,' the older woman said, making a move to leave, 'I need to go and unpack.'

'Yes, of course, but before you go – we have the room next door to the suite you originally booked. It's much smaller, obviously, but it has the same views and you'd be closer to the part of the hotel that matters to you. We'd be very happy to swap if that makes things easier for you,' she offered, hoping that Anthony wouldn't object to her spontaneity and praying that the Riverses' accommodation also had a private bathroom. 'We haven't really settled in yet, so you wouldn't be putting us to any trouble.'

Mrs Rivers seemed surprised by Elva's generosity, but quickly shook her head. 'It's very kind of you, but the last thing I actually want is to be in those rooms again. My daughter died while we were living here, and my husband thought that coming back would help us both to come to terms with what happened . . .'

The revelation shocked Elva, but she sensed that Celia Rivers wasn't a woman who would welcome sympathy from a stranger. 'And you don't agree?' she said, suppressing an urge to ask for the girl's name, or for any other small detail that might make the conversation less cold and impersonal.

'No. I don't want to remember her at all.' The words slipped out before Mrs Rivers could stop them, and this time she obviously regretted her honesty. 'I'm sorry, that sounded heartless and I didn't mean it, but even now, all these years later, I can't mourn her without feeling guilty. I let her down, you see. Do you have children, Mrs Pratt?'

'No, not yet.'

'Then perhaps you don't understand. No mother wants a room that overlooks her child's grave, but Charles is obsessed.' Elva longed to ask how the girl had died, but her own boldness was no match for Mrs Rivers's and the moment passed. 'Anyway, we have Charles's nurse with us, so we need the suite of rooms, but thank you for the offer. It really was very kind of you.'

Elva stood aside to let her pass, unable to decide if the conversation had been confiding or downright hostile. Either way, it scarcely boded well for a light-hearted murder-mystery party: most of the people here so far seemed to be genuinely in mourning. Her heart sank even further as Browning beckoned her over from reception.

'This is very good of you, Mrs Pratt. I couldn't answer any of Mrs Grayson's questions, and when I telephoned the police station, no one would tell me anything. I'll take you through to the kitchen.'

She followed him down a dark corridor towards the rear of the hotel. Except for the oak-framed leaded windows that were everywhere, this part of the building paid little heed to Tudor Close's artfully manufactured period feel. Updated in the mid-thirties, when a dozen more bedrooms had been added in a new wing, the kitchens were all-electric and boasted every type of appliance and convenience imaginable. That said, the scene that greeted Elva might have been the same in any country house over the past hundred years: steaming copper pans on a vast stove; three young kitchen maids peeling vegetables and stirring sauces; and, in the middle of it all, the archetypal figure of the cook, dressed in white with a mob cap, ruddy-faced and covered in flour, chopping onions on the long wooden table. An empty brandy glass placed discreetly by her side was the only indication that anything was wrong, and Elva wondered how Mrs Grayson could be working so efficiently, but when she watched more closely there was something frenzied about the cook's movements, as though to stop would be to let in a reality that she had no wish to face.

Browning cleared his throat and gently put a hand on her arm. 'Mrs Pratt's here, Dorothy.'

If she hadn't been told, Elva would never have guessed that Ethel Silver and Dorothy Grayson were related. The cook was as heavily built as her sister was sparrow-like, and an inopportune reference to Jack Sprat ran through Elva's mind before decorum could stop it. When Mrs Grayson looked up, it was obvious that she had been crying, but her expression was hard-set and bore very little resemblance to the gentle face that Elva remembered from her visits to the sweet shop on the high street. 'I'm very sorry for your loss,' she said with sincerity. 'It must have been a terrible shock for you. Are you sure you should be working?'

'Thank you, madam, but it's best to keep busy. Ethel wouldn't thank me for letting people down. Always had a sense of duty, she did. I wished she hadn't, sometimes. Things might have been better for her.' She stopped what she was doing and sat down heavily on one of the chairs that Browning had brought forward for them before returning to his reception desk. 'Reg says it was you who found her?'

'Yes. Well, my husband, really. We called in to collect something, but there was no sign of your sister so he went to look for her.'

'What happened to her?'

Elva shared what little she knew, trying to soften the details of the murder while supplying enough information to satisfy Dorothy Grayson. 'The police think it was a burglary,' she concluded, falling back on the same half-truth that she had criticised Anthony for; somehow, it seemed the kindest explanation in the absence of anything more definite, and she found herself compounding the story with her own wishful thinking. 'They're sure it happened quickly,' she said. 'Someone must have surprised her, so I doubt she'll have known much about it. I hope that brings you some comfort.'

Mrs Grayson shook her head, more in disbelief than denial. 'We had our ups and downs over the years. Families do, don't they? But we were always there for each other when it mattered – except this time. I can't help feeling I've let her down.'

It was the second time in only a few minutes that Elva had heard such an expression of guilt, and the similarity of the words brought an odd sort of kinship to the very different women who had expressed them. 'You couldn't possibly have known this would happen,' she said gently. 'There's only one person to blame for your sister's death, and that's whoever killed her.'

'She should never have bought that shop,' Mrs Grayson said, oblivious to Elva's reassurance. 'I warned her that no good would come of it.'

'Why do you say that?'

'When something looks too good to be true, it usually is. That's all I'm saying.' Infuriatingly, she was true to her word, and Elva was left frustrated by another half-story as the cook got up and went over to the kettle. 'I'll make your tea now, and there are some mince pies just out of the oven. It's very good of you to take the trouble to come and see me.' She bustled about, preparing the tray, and Elva stood up to take it. 'Are you sure you'll manage? I can get one of the girls to run this upstairs for you.'

'No, don't bother them. I can see how busy you all are.' She looked around at the plentiful supplies, remembering that the hotel had its own farm and dairy. 'Everything smells wonderful, by the way, and you're working miracles, especially under the circumstances.'

Elva had been referring to the sadness of Miss Silver's death, but the cook misunderstood. 'The rationing's a challenge, especially at Christmas, but you've just got to use a bit of imagination. Let me put that light on for you so you can find your way out.' She flicked a switch and the passageway back to reception was suddenly flooded with light. It was obviously where the staff kept their personal belongings, with a row of coat hooks, a shoe rack and an umbrella stand, and Elva stared at the wall in surprise. There on one of the hooks, hanging with a good wool coat that looked as if it would fit Mrs Grayson, was a red headscarf.

She hurried back to their room with the tray. Anthony had obviously not been idle in her absence. He was sitting on the bed, scribbling on the notepad and surrounded by torn-out pages, all covered in lists and diagrams. 'We must find out more about . . .' she began, but he held up his hand to interrupt her.

'I've got it!' he said. 'It's simple. We treat it like a board game and make the guests the suspects.' Still preoccupied by her own thoughts, Elva took a moment to catch up with what he was telling her. 'I'm not explaining this very well,' he apologised, misunderstanding her lack of response, 'and we're not there yet by any means, but I've had some ideas that might work. Think of the ground floor here as the playing board, with all the rooms laid out and the players – suspects, guests, whatever you want to call them – moving from one room to another. It's more interactive that way. We can make up a story around it, but we give everyone a chance to be part of the mystery – that's what people want from a game like this. And it actually feels more authentic than what we usually do with the actors because the guests are *involved* in the mystery and not just spectators.'

'This whole experience is turning out to be *very* authentic,' Elva said with feeling. 'We've both come far too close to a murder mystery today. So where does the whodunit part come in?'

'Hang on. I haven't quite finished yet. Originally, I was thinking that we should at least find someone to be the body, just to kick things off. Surely that wouldn't be too much to ask, even if he or she wasn't an actor? Then it occurred to me that there would be so many more possibilities if we didn't have a body at all – a physical body, I mean.'

'You've lost me now. We *always* have a body.'

'That's because we always have actors. This time, it's got to be different. The only thing the players know at the start of the game is that someone's been murdered – we can give him or her a name, flesh it out a bit, but we don't say where or how they were killed. That gives them more to guess.'

'But it could go on for ever. How would they ever know?'

'Because we put limits on it. The number of suspects will be determined by how many guests want to play. Then we choose the rooms downstairs that we want to use, and move between them as the game goes on to make it a bit more theatrical. Last but not least, we'll select some possible weapons – half a dozen or so should do, made up from what we can find around the hotel. For a start, we've got the prop gun we brought with us for the murder we'd planned with the actors . . .'

'A candlestick or a knife shouldn't be too hard to find,' Elva added, as excited now by the idea as he was, 'and there's bound to be some poison in the garden shed. We could put it all under the tree outside the dining room so it's the first thing they see when they come down to breakfast.'

'Steady – we don't want to put them off their bacon and eggs.'

'Oh, I'll stick a bit of tinsel round it. Perhaps we could attach some labels with the suspects' names on – something playful to set the tone for the day and get the guests thinking about the murder they're expecting.'

'Good idea! The important thing, though, is that we make it a game of probability and deduction, not imagination. The players rule things *out* rather than making them up.'

'It's a much better idea than asking the guests to take

on roles that the actors were going to play, which is what I thought you were suggesting. It would have taken far too long to brief them, and they might not be any good at it.'

'Exactly. The other option was for you and I to tell them the story and make them guess at the end, but that isn't very interesting. They might as well stay in their rooms and read a detective novel.'

'How do we come to the solution, though?' Elva asked, after thinking things through for a moment. 'Is it as arbitrary as you and I deciding whodunit and waiting for someone to guess correctly? How do we give them a chance to eliminate the red herrings?'

'That's the bit I haven't worked out yet. We *could* put clues or riddles for each red herring around the hotel. The first person to guess them all and tick them off will be left with the solution.'

'That's a lot of riddles to write before tomorrow,' Elva said doubtfully. 'Call me selfish, but I'd like us to have some of Christmas Eve to ourselves.'

'Yes, so would I.'

Elva looked at the alarm clock on her bedside table. 'Why don't you go and try the piano out? It always helps you to think, and soon we'll have to start changing for dinner.'

'All right. I won't be long.'

'While you're down there, try to get a bit more information out of Browning. That's what I was going to tell you.' She recounted her recent conversations, finishing with what she had seen on her way out of the kitchen. 'Browning must surely know more about the Riverses and their daughter's death,' she reasoned, 'and is there a *Mr* Grayson around, I wonder? If that red headscarf was the one I saw in the car on the high street, he might well have been the customer leaving Miss Silver's shop.'

'Mrs Grayson involved in her own sister's death? Surely not.'

She shrugged. 'Stranger things have happened. Go and do some sleuthing.'

He was back in a jiffy, but with very little news. 'No sign of Browning, I'm afraid. He must be taking a break before the dinner shift. On a brighter note, the Steinway sounds as sweet as a nut, so at least the music should run smoothly.' He glanced over her shoulder at the drawing she was making on the back of a menu card. 'Why are you defacing Tudor Close's stationery?'

'I'm sketching out the room plan. If we're going to use downstairs as our playing board, I thought it might help to visualise it.' She finished with a flourish and passed it over to him. 'It's only rough at the moment, but you get the idea. Dining room, red lounge, billiard room, conservatory, great log room – all the places we'll use to bring the story to life. I've kept the gun room, too. I know they don't keep guns in it these days, but I thought it was more sinister than calling it the boot room.' Anthony looked down at her work, eleven squares and rectangles of varying sizes, each boldly labelled. The rooms were linked by a path of dots and arrows, suggesting the route that the guests would take in moving between them. 'What do you think?' she asked. ' Does it help?'

He didn't answer immediately, but his face lit up. 'See it like this and it really *could* be a board game.' The idea was obvious as soon as he had voiced it. 'Elva, it's wonderful. That's what we should do. I don't mean here,' he added, noticing her confusion. 'We'll cobble something together for tomorrow – a glass or two of claret at lunchtime and no one will care whodunit. But we should work on this together when we get home. A detective board game – no one's ever done that before. It could be something really special.'

'It would certainly give you something to think about during those endless hours on the drilling machine,' she said, pleased to see him so excited. 'And you never know, it might even make us a few bob.'

Anthony picked her up and swung her round, then helped himself to one of the forgotten mince pies from the tray. 'To *Murder at Tudor Close*,' he said, chinking his cup against hers. 'Game on!'

3
MISS SILVER MAKES A 'SUGGESTION'

Anthony was relieved that the music came back to him so naturally, as half his mind was still working through the idea that he and Elva had come up with shortly before dinner. He sat at the piano, playing a set-list of tunes that had been fresh and new when he last did this for a living, and it pleased him to see how popular they still were. There would be no wartime songs tonight.

The Tudor's low-ceilinged dining room looked at its most hospitable in the mellow candlelight. Glasses and cutlery sparkled, and garlands of greenery had been hung from the beams, giving a faint scent of pine that mixed with the wood smoke and richly spiced cooking to create the very essence of Christmas. Outside, the snow had finally stopped and the dark-shrouded drifts in the garden created a magical, mysterious stage set. Anthony looked around as he played, appraising the guests who would take part in the following day's entertainment. The handful of couples whom he hadn't yet met seemed relatively normal, thank goodness, talking and laughing quietly with each other and apparently keen to enjoy every moment of their

Christmas holiday. In the far corner, the Reverend Teal, vicar of St Margaret's, sat quietly alone, lost in his own thoughts, but as far as Anthony could see he was the only solitary diner; the mysterious Mrs Threadgold was obviously having a tray in her room.

He glanced over to Elva, seated by the door, and noticed that she, too, was enjoying her first opportunity to observe their fellow guests without having to engage. Not surprisingly, her attention seemed to be taken primarily by the Riverses, who were at a table for three in the centre of the room. Anthony had been surprised to see their nurse dining with them; usually, any travelling staff at the Tudor ate separately, but perhaps that was too much trouble now for Browning and his depleted team – or perhaps Mrs Rivers simply welcomed some female companionship as an antidote to her overbearing husband. He began to play 'All the Things You Are', and was gratified when Elva looked across immediately and caught his eye; it had always been one of their favourites.

The dining-room doors opened to admit a latecomer, and Anthony was suddenly conscious that the piano grew steadily in volume as the conversation in the room fell away. The new arrival was a colonel in the Canadian army and he wore military dress rather than black tie, but it wasn't that which was making everyone stare as much as the colour of his skin. There was an excruciating silence and it was left to Browning – acting as head waiter – to show the Colonel to his table and take his order for a drink. When the whisky and soda arrived, he raised it to the room and wished everyone a happy Christmas. Anthony admired his courage, then immediately rebuked himself for falling into the same category as the other diners; no man should need courage to walk into a room full of his peers, especially one who had left his own country to come and fight for theirs. Spontaneously, he switched to an old Guy Lombardo tune – the only Canadian musician he could think of – and received a nod of appreciation from the floor.

He played through to his allotted break, then went over to join Elva. 'You haven't lost your touch,' she said, sliding a glass of wine across the table. 'It's so lovely to hear you play again. You never go near the piano at home these days.'

Anthony shrugged. 'It's not the same as having an audience and doing it properly. I don't want music to be just a hobby. I love it too much for that.'

'Well, everyone certainly appreciates it. Even the Riverses cheered up for a while.'

'Then my work is done.' He noticed her untouched place

setting. 'You shouldn't have waited, though. You must be starving by now.'

'I'd much rather eat with you. Browning said he'd bring our food over as soon as you'd finished the first set.'

The manager was as good as his word. Within seconds, a fish soup appeared in front of them, followed by a savoury meat pie made with potato pastry.

'The food might not be as fancy as it used to be,' Elva said, putting down her knife and fork, 'but my God that was tasty.'

Anthony nodded, wiping his plate round with the last piece of bread. 'You certainly wouldn't know Mrs Grayson was grieving. I wonder what she'll conjure up for Christmas Day?'

'I don't think I mind. It's just nice to let someone else worry about what to do with another bloody marrow. Do you want dessert now or when you've finished?'

'Let's save it for later. I've got to start again in a few minutes.'

He savoured the last drop of wine, smiling at the Colonel, who was heading towards the door. To Anthony's surprise, he stopped by their table and raised his cap to Elva. 'Good evening, ma'am,' he said. 'I hate to disturb you, but I just wanted to let your husband know how much I'm enjoying his music tonight.'

'Be my guest,' Elva said, obviously charmed.

'It's a long time since I heard the piano played as beautifully as that, so thank you. Can I buy you a drink, just to show my appreciation?'

'Only if you'll have one with us,' Anthony said, turning a chair round from the table behind them. 'Please, sit down. I'm Anthony, and this is my wife, Elva.'

'What an unusual name.' He shook hands with them both and took the chair that was offered. 'Will Colman. Delighted to meet you, but I really don't want to intrude.'

'You're not. I've got to go back to the piano in a minute, but I'm sure my wife would appreciate the company.' He winked at her when the Colonel wasn't looking. 'Mr Browning was telling us that you've been here for a couple of years now?'

'A bit longer than that, actually. The regiment came over at Christmas in 1939. I've been here on and off since then.'

'And what do you do?'

'Mainly coastal defence work and training. We've got a big operation coming up, so it's good for the boys to have some time off over Christmas. I bet the Grange is lively tonight.'

'Is that where the mess is?' Colman nodded. 'You're not tempted to join them?'

'No. I'm afraid I've reached the age where some civilised company and an early night are what I crave most. And Mr Browning was good enough to invite me to dine here over Christmas.'

Anthony wondered if the awkward reception Colman had received earlier counted as civilised company, but the Colonel seemed to have taken it in his stride so he said nothing. They chatted about the regiment's duties for a while until Anthony caught a pointed look in Browning's eye when he brought the drinks over. 'I'd better go and start the second set,' he said apologetically. 'I hope we'll get to talk more across the weekend.'

When he got back to the piano, he found a note on the keyboard requesting that he play one of Mozart's piano sonatas. The note was anonymous, but it was a piece that he knew well and loved, and its relaxed tone seemed appropriate for this stage of the evening, so he began it straight away. He had barely got through the first few bars when there was a disturbance at the Riverses' table and everyone turned to look. Someone had knocked over a glass, and in the recriminations that followed, Anthony could see that Mrs Rivers, in particular, was distressed. After another bitter exchange of words, she stood and left the restaurant, quickly followed by her husband's nurse. Rivers himself stayed seated at the table, staring into his wine glass, and in the corner the Reverend Teal rose to his feet, as if intending to join him; the vicar hesitated, then changed his mind and sat back down again, and the atmosphere in the dining room gradually returned to normal.

Anthony curtailed the Mozart, reverting to the livelier tunes of the first set and throwing in a carol or two in an attempt to lift the mood. In the old days, the tables would have been pushed back for dancing and Christmas seen in by a joyful crowd; now, they were an older, wearier nation, it seemed, and the guests drifted off with very little ceremony to wait for midnight in their rooms or over a nightcap at the bar. That was what four years of war had done, Anthony thought, glad to bring the entertainment to an end – so much for the famous community spirit. 'What on earth was that business with the Riverses about?' he asked, rejoining Elva at their table.

'I'm not pointing the finger, but it seemed to be the music that did it. She was asking him to make you stop playing, said she couldn't bear it. I wondered if it reminded her of her daughter. What made you choose Mozart?'

'I didn't.' He told her about the note on the piano.

'And it wasn't signed?'

'No.'

'Do you think someone asked for it deliberately because they knew it would upset her?'

'Perhaps. I wonder if Browning knows anything about it?'

But he didn't. 'I'm sorry, sir. Nobody gave it to me to deliver. Can I get you some dessert?'

Anthony looked at Elva, pleased to see that she seemed as unenthusiastic as he was. 'No, thank you,' she said. 'We need to head upstairs and do some planning for tomorrow, but thank Mrs Grayson for us. That was a lovely meal, especially under the circumstances.'

They left the dining room and walked out into the hallway. 'How did you enjoy your military escort?' Anthony asked.

'Very much. He's an interesting man, and he fought in the last war, too, you know. He was telling me how much easier it's been for black Canadians to enlist this time round – no more segregated battalions. Haven't we come a long way?' The sarcasm in her voice was tangible. 'And he was a friend of Miss Silver's, too. He told me how welcoming she was when he first arrived here. Her death has really upset him, I think.'

'You told him?'

'I didn't have to. He already knew.'

'How, I wonder?'

Elva shrugged. 'He didn't say, but I assumed one of the staff told him – he's been here a while, and he seems to know them all. We talked a lot about losing people, and how strange it is that we should all be so shocked by one death in the context of everything else that's happening. Strange but comforting, somehow.' She smiled at him. 'He sounded a bit like you after you've read a crime novel – all hell-bent on justice.'

'Except there's nothing made up about Miss Silver's death. I'm sorry if I lumbered you with a depressing conversation. It doesn't sound very Christmassy.'

'It wasn't, but it was interesting. And on a brighter note, I've got our first murder weapon.'

She beckoned him closer and opened her clutch bag, and Anthony saw the syringe nestled in between the lipstick and the comb. 'Where on earth did you find that?'

'Under the Riverses' table. It must have fallen out of Nurse Blanchett's bag. It's empty, before you ask. No poisons.'

'I'm quite curious about that nurse, you know. Odd that she was dining with them. I wondered if she and Professor Rivers are closer than they should be?'

Elva looked doubtful. 'Do you think so? She's more likely to be close to his wife, I'd have said.' She laughed

83

at the shocked expression on his face. 'Don't be so straitlaced. It happens, and those two women didn't stop talking all night before the incident. If he's as domineering as he seems, I don't blame her.' She found the room key and paused at the foot of the stairs. 'Shall we collect some more murder weapons for tomorrow before we go up? I've warned Browning that's what we're doing, so he won't think we're stealing the silver when I help myself to the heaviest candlestick I can find.'

'Good idea. There's a spanner in the car, too. I'll go and fetch that and the other suitcase. See you back at the room.'

Outside, a world of perfect stillness had settled around the hotel, hushed and expectant, and Anthony couldn't help but think that nature was doing a much better job of honouring the Christmas spirit than anyone inside. Their car proved to be a richer source of deathly paraphernalia than he had imagined: as well as the spanner, he found a rope and an axe, both there in case of emergencies that never transpired, and took them all triumphantly inside, hoping that he wouldn't meet anyone of a nervous disposition on the stairs.

Elva had done well, too. On the rug in front of the fire, the syringe and prop revolver now sat in company with an ornate silver candlestick that would have graced any altar;

an unpleasant-looking kitchen knife; a poker; and a bottle of rat poison, handily marked with a skull and crossbones. 'That should do nicely,' Anthony said, adding his haul to hers. 'There are still a few people milling around downstairs, so we should wait a bit before taking them down to the tree. We don't want to ruin the surprise.'

It was a quarter to midnight, so they changed into warmer clothes and threw the windows wide open, waiting for the church clock to strike the hour. 'It's good to have the bells back,' Elva said, when the moment came. 'It feels hopeful, somehow, no matter how bad things get.'

Anthony pulled her close and kissed her. 'Things don't feel bad at all right now,' he said. 'Happy Christmas.'

'Happy Christmas.'

They stood by the window until the fresh night air became piercing rather than exhilarating, then drew the curtains and built up the fire to last while they went downstairs. Armed with their motley collection, they ventured out onto the landing and headed for the staircase that led directly down to the old hall by the dining room. 'I feel a bit like Santa Claus's wicked sister,' Elva whispered, 'delivering the presents that no one would ever want.'

'Oh, I don't know. I'm very proud of my noose.' Anthony winked, and held up the hangman's knot that had transformed an innocent coil of rope into something far more sinister. 'All that time in the Scouts paid off.'

They arranged the weapons under the tree, interspersing them with the wrapped gifts already there, and stood back to gauge the effect. 'We still haven't decided exactly what we're going to do with them,' Elva said, turning out the labels to show the character names that Anthony had invented, 'but they look good.'

'That's the main thing. We'll worry about the rest in the morning. I've had enough tension for one day.'

He turned for the stairs but Elva caught his hand. 'Let's go and say goodnight to Browning first. There's a light on in reception so he must still be up.'

Anthony groaned. 'You just want to quiz him about the Riverses and Mrs Grayson,' he said. 'Couldn't we leave it until the morning?'

'He'll be on his own now, and it won't take a minute to ask him how the Riverses' daughter died – he must have been with the family when it happened.'

'Should we be prying like that? She might have had a terrible illness, and it's not really our business to start raking up bad memories.'

'Don't worry, I'll be tactful. I want to know how long Miss Silver has had her shop, too.'

'Fourteen years.'

She looked at him in surprise. 'How do you know that?'

'It's written above the door. "Est. 1929". I noticed it today.'

'So the same year as Tudor Close became a hotel, and just after the Riverses left. That *is* interesting.'

'Why, Miss Marple? What's the connection?'

Elva looked faintly embarrassed. 'I'm not sure yet,' she admitted. 'It just feels significant. Browning might shed more light on it.'

But it wasn't Browning at reception. As they turned the corner, they saw Charles Rivers trying to open the key cupboard behind the desk. Anthony grabbed Elva's arm and pulled her back out of sight, signalling to her to be quiet. He peered round the corner and watched as Rivers searched through all the drawers, eventually locating a bunch of keys. After several attempts, he found one that opened the cupboard, then took another key off a hook and relocked everything. Hurriedly, Anthony retreated a few steps along the corridor and began to talk loudly to Elva as if they had just arrived. By the time they turned the corner, Rivers was back on the guest side of the desk, apparently waiting to be served.

They wished him goodnight and carried on upstairs as if nothing had happened. 'What the hell was he up to?' Elva asked when they were safely back in their room.

'Looking for a spare key to number seven would be my guess,' Anthony said. 'He's obviously determined to get in there by fair means or foul. What can he possibly want badly enough from that room to risk getting caught?'

'I don't know, but do you think we should warn Mrs Threadgold?'

'And say what? She'd think we were mad. Better to find Browning and let him deal with it.'

'But we've got no idea where to look. Browning might not even live on the premises.'

They were still undecided when they heard the door to number seven open and close, followed by creaking floorboards as someone retreated along the landing. 'What if that's him?' Elva whispered in a panic.

'It can't be. That was someone leaving.' Anthony went to the door and opened it a crack, just in time to see a man heading for the stairs. Down the corridor, in Mrs Threadgold's suite, he heard a key turn in the lock and two bolts pulled firmly across. 'I *think* it was the Reverend Teal,' he said in answer to Elva's questioning stare, 'but God knows why at this time of night. We don't have to worry about Rivers having a key, though. That door's firmly bolted, so he can't get in.'

They settled down in the armchairs, lost in thought for a while as the firelight flickered companionably on the ceiling. 'Why don't you have one of those cigars?' Elva suggested. 'I have a horrible feeling that this is as much peace and quiet as we're going to get, so you might as well enjoy them while you can.'

'Good idea, but only if you open something, too.' He went over to the chaise longue at the bottom of the bed, where Elva had arranged their gifts to each other, and selected a small square box. 'Chocolates and cigars – a suitable tribute to Miss Silver, don't you think?'

He undid the ribbon and slipped the tissue off the cigars, and a white envelope fell to the floor. 'It must be our Christmas card,' Elva said quietly. 'I've still got hers in my handbag. How sad.' She picked the card up to open it, then hesitated. 'Hang on – this isn't for us. It's addressed to Professor Rivers.'

'What?' She held it up to show him. 'So does that mean . . .'

'. . . that there were two boxes to be collected and we've got the wrong one? Looks like it. In which case, was it the Riverses we saw at the shop?'

'She wasn't wearing a red hat in reception.'

'She wasn't wearing a hat at all. Didn't that strike you as

strange in this weather? I wondered about it at the time.'

'In any case, we now know that Miss Silver knew the Riverses well enough to send a Christmas card. I suppose we should give this to them in the morning.'

Elva nodded reluctantly. 'Yes, I suppose we should. Or we could just open it by mistake.'

She drew inverted commas in the air and Anthony grinned. 'My thoughts exactly.' He tore the envelope open and read the message out loud, looking puzzled. '"Fifteen Christmases. Time for you to make amends." That's it. There's nothing else but her signature.'

'As threats go, it's a very genteel one, but still a threat, wouldn't you say?'

'Definitely. Enough to put him firmly in the frame for Miss Silver's murder – except, of course, he never received it.' Anthony scratched his head, thinking about the message in the card. 'It does clearly suggest that she knew something, though, and perhaps it's not the first time she's called him out. Interesting that it's just to him. There's no mention of Mrs Rivers on the card or the envelope.'

'Well, we should definitely let the police know about it.'

'I'll telephone Inspector Clough tomorrow. And of course, if we've got Rivers's card, they've probably got one for us. It might make them suspicious, I suppose.'

Elva yawned. 'I'm too tired to worry about that tonight. I just want to go to bed while the room's still warm enough to face getting undressed.'

'Good idea.' Anthony changed into his pyjamas and switched all the lamps off. A sliver of moonlight shone brilliantly through a gap in the curtains, and he went to the window to take one last look at the magic of the night-time snow. It cloaked the churchyard, bending branches and bushes low to the ground and lying in swathes against the gravestones. He gave an involuntary shudder, thinking of the young girl buried there, just a stone's throw from her parents' old home. 'You're right, we must find out how the Riverses' daughter died and when,' he said into the silence. 'Was it their fault, I wonder? Is that why she felt guilty? Is that what they need to make amends for?' But there was no answer. Elva was already fast asleep.

4
THE REVEREND TEAL

The very thought of getting out of bed made Elva shiver, but someone had to be first to brave the cold and she knew it wouldn't be Anthony. The church clock finished striking eight as she threw the covers back and grabbed her dressing gown, then tiptoed across the floor to pull back the curtains on a perfect Christmas morning. Sunlight glistened on the ridges, and her first glimpse of Tudor Close in daylight didn't disappoint: the weather-beaten walls of flint, the mossy ancient timber – taken, it was said, from Tudor warships – blended beautifully with the snow to create a timeless image that would have graced any greetings card.

A polite knock at the door signalled the arrival of their morning tea. Elva poured two cups, glad to cradle the warmth in her hands, then shook Anthony awake. 'Did inspiration for the murder-mystery strike during the night?' she asked. 'I'm afraid I was dead to the world.'

'Me too, and when I did wake up I was thinking about Miss Silver. The riddle idea was probably the best one, but we've left it far too late to write all those.'

'We could give the carol service a miss and do it after breakfast.'

'But you love the carol service. No, the thing that kept coming back to me in the early hours was that we shouldn't be doing it at all. Genuinely, I mean, and not just to get ourselves out of a hole. The very idea of a murder mystery seems in poor taste. We could take Browning to one side and appeal to his better nature. Anyway, by the time we've had the carol service and Christmas lunch, we'll be halfway through the afternoon. A game of charades should do it, and we can run those in our sleep.'

In her heart, Elva agreed with him, although it concerned her that they were accepting hospitality on false pretences. 'Still, it isn't our fault that there's been a real murder,' she said, wrestling out loud with her conscience. 'How could anyone have foreseen that?'

'Exactly. And as long as we entertain people with the music and some party games, Browning will be happy. It'll be a much more enjoyable atmosphere all round if we're not constantly worried about upsetting someone.'

There was a tempting smell of toast and bacon on the air, and now that their decision was made, they dressed for breakfast with a lighter heart. 'We'll have to get rid of all that stuff under the tree,' Elva said as they left their room.

'Let's do it as soon as we've had a chance to . . .'

The rest of the sentence was lost in a piercing scream from the staircase. 'God, what now?' Anthony groaned, quickening his pace along the corridor.

When they turned the corner, they saw Mrs Rivers and Nurse Blanchett standing at the top of the stairs, staring at something straight ahead, a look of absolute horror on their faces. The reason for their distress became obvious as Anthony and Elva approached the landing. The noose that they had nestled so innocently among the presents under the Christmas tree now hung from the rafters, thrown over one of the beams to transform the hotel's elegant staircase into a sinister, makeshift gallows. 'Get it down!' the nurse shouted, putting her arm around Mrs Rivers and turning her gently away. 'Get the damned thing down!'

Anthony rushed to help, but the noose was just out of his reach so he continued down to the hall to find a member of staff. There was a kerfuffle while someone tried to balance a chair on the step, then – when that proved impossible – went to look for a ladder. By that time, a few early risers had emerged from the dining room to see what was going on. To Elva's surprise, the grim tableau seemed to amuse rather than disturb them; clearly they thought that it was part of the entertainment they had been promised, and assumed that Mrs Rivers and Nurse Blanchett were in on the joke. The surreal collection of murder weapons under the tree pricked her conscience; if they hadn't left the rope in the hallway, this would never have happened, and she went over to Mrs Rivers to make amends. 'Perhaps you should go back to your room while we get this sorted out,' she said gently, leading her away from the stairs. 'I'll find Mr Browning and ask him to bring you some breakfast there if you'd prefer?'

Mrs Rivers shook her head. 'I don't want anything to eat,' she insisted, but her companion overruled her.

'You've got to have something, Celia,' she said, kindly but firmly, 'and that's a good idea. Go back to the room now and I'll be there in a minute.' She turned gratefully to Elva. 'That's thoughtful of you. Thank you. This has been a terrible shock for her.'

'It's the least I can do,' Elva said, meaning every word of it. 'Is Professor Rivers there with her?'

'Yes, he wasn't up to an early start. He has fewer and fewer good days now. I can't help feeling that it will be a blessing when it finally comes.'

She walked away, leaving Elva to read between the lines. When she got back to Anthony, the crisis was over: Colonel Colman was passing through with some other officers, and they made short work of hoisting one of their party up onto broad shoulders to reach the noose. Colman passed the rope to Anthony, touched his hat to Elva, then headed outside to the officers' mess for breakfast just as Browning arrived with a stepladder. 'Thank goodness for that,' he said, looking at the rope with distaste. 'It gave me the shock of my life when I came in early this morning.'

'You saw it then?' Anthony said. 'Why did you leave it there?'

'I assumed it was part of what you were planning,' Browning admitted, looking mortified. 'Mrs Pratt had warned me that you were collecting murder weapons and I saw all the others under the tree. I did think the noose was rather insensitive, if I'm honest, but I didn't like to interfere. So you really didn't put it there?'

'Absolutely not,' Elva said, frowning at Anthony, who looked as if he half-wished they'd thought of it. 'We left it under the tree with everything else. It's a horrible, gruesome thing. I can see why Mrs Rivers was so upset.'

'It's more personal than that, I'm afraid.'

'Oh?'

Browning lowered his voice. 'Their daughter hanged herself. It was a terrible time. She was only fourteen.'

Elva was too shocked to speak, which was probably just as well, because her first reaction was to wonder at Browning's heartlessness: knowing what he knew, surely he should have felt compelled to take the noose down, regardless of how it affected any plans for a murder-mystery game? Perhaps what Rivers had said at check-in was fair after all: Browning really did hold a grudge against them.

'I'm so sorry,' Anthony said. 'We'd never have included a rope if we'd known.' He looked doubtfully towards the tree. 'Perhaps we'd better get rid of all that. It feels a little crass under the circumstances.'

'And for Mrs Grayson's sake, too,' Elva added, seizing the moment to introduce their change of plan.

'If you're sure, Mrs Pratt, that might be best. I'll have it all cleared away. I didn't like to suggest it when you've gone to such trouble . . .'

'It's no trouble,' Anthony said quickly. 'We'll do something more tactful this afternoon.'

'Thank you, sir. Much appreciated.'

'Why did she do it?' Elva asked. 'The Riverses' daughter, I mean.'

'No one knows. Now, if you'll excuse me . . .'

They watched him go. 'I doubt that *very* much,' Elva said

cynically. 'I bet the Riverses know, even if they kept it to themselves.'

'And I bet that's what Miss Silver was referring to in her Christmas message.'

They carried on to the dining room, where breakfast was laid out in silver serving dishes along the sideboard. Anthony helped them both to bacon, toast and mushrooms while Elva poured the coffee, and they sat down at their table from the night before. 'Who on earth can have put that rope there?' Elva said.

'Well, we left Rivers on his own down here...'

'Surely he wouldn't terrorise his own wife like that.'

'... and the Reverend Teal was wandering the corridors after midnight. Mrs Grayson and her staff must have come in early for breakfast, and the soldiers seem to pass through whenever they feel like it.' He stirred his coffee thoughtfully. 'Let's face it, anyone could have come down here to do it. The rope was just sitting under the tree.'

'Not my best idea, in hindsight.'

'You weren't to know.'

'We seem to be saying that a lot this Christmas.'

They headed to church after breakfast, using the gate in the boundary wall that separated Tudor Close from St Margaret's graveyard. The air was exhilaratingly crisp, and Elva hoped that it might help them to think more clearly. In the distance, on Beacon Hill, she could see the familiar silhouette of Rottingdean windmill, a striking landmark for ships out at sea and visible from so many places in the village; this morning, its black sails and boarding looked even more dramatic than usual against the white hillside.

St Margaret's stood opposite the green, and the peace of its setting belied the violence of its past: here and there, rose-coloured patches on the walls recalled centuries-old fire damage from the sacking of the village, when all those who took refuge in the bell tower had been burned to death. The graveyard was old and rambling, divided into different sections by flint walls and archways, and some of the memorials went back hundreds of years, the names of those they honoured now faded or covered in moss. 'Look,' Elva said, squeezing Anthony's arm as they walked round to the entrance. 'Rivers is over there. That must be their daughter's grave. We should go and have a look after the service. I'm surprised she was allowed to be buried here at all if it was a suicide, though.'

'It'll be the old "balance of the mind disturbed" thing, I suppose. Teal's obviously a particularly compassionate vicar.'

He certainly seemed to be a popular one. The congregation had turned out in force, boosted by soldiers and the hotel, and Elva wondered if it was from a genuine desire to worship at Christmas, from the desperation of war, or simply from the fact that the village was too small to risk offending the parson. She and Anthony took a pew near the pulpit, overlooked by a bust of the Reverend Hooker, Rottingdean's famous smuggling vicar, who had carried contraband through the underground tunnels that connected the village's larger properties, including the original Tudor Close farmhouse. From where they sat, Elva had the perfect view of her favourite part of the church. She had feared that the stained-glass windows – made by William Morris to designs by Burne-Jones – might have been removed for safekeeping during the war, but they were still in place, protected by boarding which had been taken down for the Christmas service, and the morning sun streamed through them, showing the deep blues and flaming reds at their most intense and brilliant. The colours and lead work would have made the windows beautiful in their own right, but they seemed even more special to her because the artist who designed them had made his home in the village and worshipped in the church. Above the altar, the east window was a triptych of archangels: Gabriel and the Annunciation; Michael slaying the dragon; and Raphael, healer and guardian of young children, holding the hand of a little boy who looked up at him with an expression of absolute trust that Elva had always found deeply moving.

'I'm surprised they didn't ask you to play the organ as well,' she whispered, noticing Anthony wince as a florid solo during the first carol struck several false notes.

He smiled. 'I think you've got to live in the village for at least a hundred years before they let you do that.'

There was the usual shuffling and clearing of throats as everyone took their seats again and looked expectantly towards the pulpit. The Reverend Teal must be in his late sixties by now, Elva supposed, and he had aged since they were last here; as he climbed up to the lectern, he looked very frail. 'In the beginning was the Word, and the Word was with God,' he began, and she was pleasantly surprised to hear the deep, attractive voice of old and not the strained, feeble tone that his appearance had led her to expect.

The service moved on through the familiar pattern of readings and carols, but somehow Teal succeeded in making the story sound new and fresh. As he spoke with conviction about the lasting relevance of the Christmas message and the painful absence of loved ones at a time of shared celebration, Elva could see that she wasn't the only person to be touched by his sincerity. 'Christ the light of the world has come to dispel the darkness of our hearts,' he said, looking benevolently out across the congregation. 'In his light let us examine ourselves and confess our sins.' He paused, and one or two people reached for their hymn books, anticipating the next carol, but the Reverend Teal was far from finished. 'And those sins are deeply rooted among us,' he continued, with a new urgency to his voice. 'An appalling act of violence has shattered the peace of our village, robbing us of one of our dearest neighbours. Many of you will have known Ethel Silver. She was much loved in this community for her kindness and generosity, and we feel her loss deeply, wrenched from a world which already knows too much bloodshed in a shocking and brutal personal attack.' A stunned murmur passed through the congregation, many of whom were obviously hearing the news of Miss Silver's death for the first time.

'So much for a burglary gone wrong,' Anthony whispered. 'What does Teal know, I wonder?'

Elva shrugged and cast her eyes across the rows behind, relieved to see that Dorothy Grayson didn't seem to be in the church to hear such an unflinching account of her sister's death. 'One of us here today has broken the most sacred of all commandments,' Teal continued, and an audible gasp passed up and down the rows. 'One of us has a long, dark struggle ahead to reach the light of our Maker's presence. Let us pray that he has already begun his journey.'

Instinctively, Elva looked across at the Riverses, sitting on the opposite side of the aisle. They were staring straight ahead, their expressions impossible to read, but she could see that Professor Rivers was gripping the side of the pew so tightly that his knuckles were white. 'Do you think Teal's using "he" by force of habit or does he really know who did it?' she asked. She tried to follow the vicar's gaze for a clue but he was staring fixedly at the back of the church, as if making eye contact with any of his parishioners might rob him of the strength to continue.

'And although it pains me to say it,' Teal added, lowering his voice, 'such a heinous deed was inevitable. For all her qualities, Miss Silver herself was not without sin. Which of us is?' This time he did look down, quickly scanning the rows in front of him. 'Our neighbour has brought this tragedy upon herself by her own weakness. When you turn a blind eye to evil, you are yourself complicit in it, and I include myself in that.' He turned to the altar. At first, Elva thought he was praying, but then he pointed towards the Burne-Jones panels. 'This window should have been our guide. Our brother Raphael, watching over the infant Tobias, protecting him from demons. Isn't that what we all feel so naturally in our hearts? The urge to nurture and protect the innocent and the vulnerable? Even our Lord, whose birth has brought us together today, relied on those who loved him for protection from people who would have done him harm.' Teal turned back to the congregation with an actor's perfect timing, and finished his highly unorthodox sermon with a real Old Testament flourish. 'Today of all days, let us find the courage to stand up for what we know is right and renounce the evil in our midst. Let us seek retribution for the wrongs of the past, cast out the one whose heart is black, and beg those we have failed for forgiveness. One day, we shall all be judged, and I ask you now to join me in penitence and faith. In the name of the Father, the Son and the Holy Ghost, amen.'

The silence in the church was broken only by the sound of children's voices in the street outside. 'Blimey,' Anthony muttered, 'I think Teal read the wrong briefing notes. I wouldn't call that the spirit of Christmas.'

The vicar cleared his throat and looked pointedly at the organist, an elderly woman who had obviously lost track of the running order in the shock of what she had just heard. She jumped to attention and did her best, but 'O Come All Ye Faithful' was sung half-heartedly, neither joyful nor triumphant, and the words seemed cruelly at odds with the message from the pulpit. When the last notes had died away, everyone began to file out into the snow and Elva wondered how Teal would handle the customary pleasantries with his parishioners, but he obviously wasn't in the mood to wish anyone a happy Christmas: when he left the pulpit, he went straight to the vestry at the side of the church.

'Come on,' Anthony said. 'Now's our chance to find out exactly what that was all about.'

'We can't just barge in . . .'

But Anthony had knocked at the vestry door before Elva could stop him, and she followed him reluctantly inside. The vicar was sitting at a small table, mopping his brow with a handkerchief, and the strain of the service had obviously taken its toll. He seemed exhausted – haunted was the word Elva would have used if pressed to describe the look in his eyes – but he brightened when he saw them, and his greeting seemed genuine. 'Mr and Mrs Pratt, isn't it? Reginald told me you were joining us this year. It's been far too long since you were here.'

'It has, but we're sorry to come back under such sad circumstances.'

'Yes, of course. It was you who found Miss Silver's body, I gather? That must have been a terrible shock.'

'It was. What do you know about her death?'

Teal began to prevaricate, and Anthony interrupted him. 'Please don't say that you can't tell us anything. You've just told the whole village and half the Canadian army that you know who killed Miss Silver and why – and in all fairness to her, if you're claiming that she brought it on herself, you ought to justify that with an explanation.'

Elva looked at her husband, surprised by his directness, and realised for the first time how angered he was by Miss Silver's murder. Because he was generally so even-tempered, because he made her laugh every day, even in the darkest of times, it was occasionally easy to forget how deeply he felt things.

Teal hesitated, absentmindedly turning a signet ring on his left hand. 'Very well,' he said eventually, 'but not here. It's too public.' One of his volunteers walked in with the collection plate, perfectly timed to justify his concerns. 'I'm having lunch at the Tudor. We can find somewhere to talk there if that suits you?'

'Perfectly.' Anthony smiled and fished a couple of

shillings out of his pocket to add to the plate. 'Perhaps we can persuade you to tell us who's in room seven, as well. She's quite the woman of mystery.'

'Room seven?'

'Yes, you were there late last night. We're next door and I saw you leaving.'

'I'm sorry, Mr Pratt, you're mistaken there,' Teal said, but he seemed unsettled. 'I left the hotel shortly after dinner.'

He stood up, effectively dismissing them. Anthony opened the door for Elva and they walked outside. 'Well, that was a lot easier than I expected,' he said.

'My thoughts exactly. We're still none the wiser about Mrs Threadgold's visitor, though.'

'Oh, it was definitely him.'

'But he's just denied it. And you said last night that you weren't sure.'

'I wasn't until just now. He was lying. I'd bet my life on it.'

They took a circuitous route around the churchyard, keen not to be too obvious about the grave they were searching for. 'I'm sure Professor Rivers was standing in this row,' Elva said, when they reached the section that was nearest Tudor Close and directly overlooked by their room. 'Yes, here it is. Lily Elizabeth Rivers. She died on 3 July 1926, so more than fifteen years ago.'

'And not at Christmas.' Anthony scratched his head. 'I thought you said she died while they were living at Tudor Close?'

'That's what Mrs Rivers told me. It's why they wanted those rooms.'

'But Tudor Close wasn't built in 1926.'

'How odd – unless they lived in the old farmhouse, of course.' Elva stared down at the grey stone, simple except for an exquisitely carved surround of the flower that had given the girl her name. 'Rest in peace, my darlings,' she read. 'That's odd, too. Why "darlings" plural?'

'A slip of the hand by the stone mason?'

'I doubt it. Look how skilfully everything else has been done. And remember how adamant Rivers was about getting the hotel room he'd booked. You're not telling me that he'd stand for a mistake on his daughter's headstone.' She shivered and took Anthony's arm. 'That's quite sinister, if you think about it. It's as if the grave is waiting for someone. Another question for the Reverend Teal.'

'There's quite a list building. We'd better get back to the hotel and pin him down. I don't want to be fobbed off again.'

As they turned to go, Elva looked up at Tudor Close and caught the movement of a curtain as someone stepped back from the first-floor window. She paused a moment, hoping for a glimpse of the woman who was living unseen and unheard in the rooms next to theirs, but Mrs Threadgold remained stubbornly elusive.

Browning had been waiting in the hallway to greet the guests coming back from the carol service, and he took two hot toddies from a dwindling tray and handed them over. 'Lunch is at half past one,' he said, 'so there's plenty of time to go to your room or relax down here. The fires are lit in the bar and the great log room, and these should help to warm you up.' He hesitated, as if debating how much to say. 'I gather from some of the other guests that there wasn't much cheer in the Christmas sermon?'

'That's putting it mildly,' Anthony said. 'Actually, we're hoping to have a chat with the Reverend before lunch. Is there somewhere private we could talk?'

'You're very welcome to use my office. He hasn't arrived yet, but I'll let you know when he does.'

'Thank you. Has there been any word from the police about Miss Silver?'

Browning shook his head. 'No, nothing at all. I was hoping for some news, if only for Mrs Grayson's sake, but no one's been in touch with any of us.'

'Perhaps they're busy following up some leads,' Elva said encouragingly. 'I'm sure they're doing their best. Are the Riverses back from church yet?'

'Yes. They're upstairs, resting before lunch.'

'We saw their daughter's headstone in the churchyard. She obviously died before they moved to Tudor Close?'

'That's right. I think they hoped that a new house might mean a fresh start, but as far as I could see the grief moved with them. At least, for *Mrs* Rivers.'

'Where did they live before?'

'In a house called The Briars, just off the green.'

'You told us other people worked for them,' Anthony said. 'Anyone else we know?'

'Mrs Grayson was their cook and housekeeper for a long time.'

'And Miss Silver?'

Browning nodded. 'For a while, yes. She was the children's governess.'

'Children?' Elva queried. 'How many did they have?'

'Just two. Lily had a younger sister, but Professor Rivers was only their stepfather. Their real father died towards the end of the last war, and Mrs Rivers – or Latimer, as she was originally – remarried when Rose was just a baby. He adopted them both.'

'What happened to Rose?'

He shrugged. 'I've had no contact with them over the

years, and, as you probably noticed, yesterday wasn't a time for pleasantries. Shall I show you through to my office now or would you rather wait in one of the other rooms until the Reverend Teal arrives?'

'We'll pop up with our coats then wait in the bar,' Elva said. She turned to the stairs, and noticed that – except for the ill-fated rope – the murder weapons were still under the tree. 'You haven't changed your mind about this afternoon's entertainment, have you?' she asked nervously.

Browning followed her gaze to the candlestick. 'Oh no, absolutely not. I just haven't had a minute to clear those things away. Don't worry, I'll see to it now.'

'At least let us take the ones that belong to us,' Anthony offered. 'Christmas will look much more peaceful without the spanner, the axe and the gun.'

He collected them and they went upstairs to their room. 'Are you going to telephone the police about the message in Miss Silver's card?' Elva asked.

'Not yet. I'd rather go straight back down and make sure we catch the vicar. The way I see it, he holds the answers to so many questions. If he's honest with us, there'll be much more to tell Inspector Clough when we do speak to him.'

They left the offending weapons in a grisly pile on the bed and headed out again. As they turned the corner on the staircase, they saw Browning alone in the old hall, staring at something by the tree and holding the candlestick that Elva had borrowed from the dining room. He looked up when he heard them approaching, his demeanour completely unrecognisable from the man they had left just ten minutes ago. 'I didn't do it,' he said inexplicably, and there was a suppressed panic in his voice that chimed with his pale face and the desperate look in his eyes. 'Please, Mr and Mrs Pratt, you have to believe me. I found him like this when I came back from reception. I'd only been gone a minute or two...'

He tailed off and let the candlestick fall to the floor. Anthony told Elva to wait where she was but she ignored him, compelled to find out what the Christmas tree was shielding her from. She saw his hand first, instantly recognising the signet ring that she had noticed in the vestry. His arm was outstretched, as it had been when he pointed to the image of Raphael, but it was a futile gesture now, and his fingers seemed to clutch at nothing more substantial than a desperate, forlorn hope. Reluctantly, she moved forward until the whole scene was visible. The Reverend Teal lay motionless by the tree, his shirt and dog collar stained with a trickle of blood from a wound at the back of his head, the splash of scarlet on white cruelly in keeping with the colours of the season. She watched as Anthony knelt down and felt in vain for a pulse; in the end, he looked up at Browning and shook his head.

Time seemed to stand still for a moment, then Elva noticed that other people were beginning to arrive for lunch, oblivious to any trouble. The Colonel came in through the conservatory, vigorously stamping the snow off his boots until he noticed the stillness of the hallway and the horror it contained. The Riversered were clinging to one another in the doorway to the lounge, with Nurse Blanchett peering over their shoulders. Waiting staff gathered outside the dining room and one or two soldiers emerged from a game of billiards but no one spoke, and Elva began to feel as if she were present at the climax to a play, watching as each character stepped forward to take his or her curtain call. Eventually, the silence was broken by a cry from off stage. Mrs Grayson stood in the shadows of the kitchen corridor, screaming at the top of her voice as she looked first at the body and then at Browning. Elva couldn't help but think that her distress seemed much greater now than it had been yesterday at the news of her sister's murder.

'Somebody phone the police,' Anthony shouted, trying to be heard over the noise.

All eyes turned to the hotel's manager but he remained rooted to the spot, obviously in shock, and Elva found herself wondering if it was because of what he had found or what he had done. His protestations had seemed genuine enough, but there was no denying that he had been caught standing over the body with the probable murder weapon in his hands.

'For God's sake, man, do as he says,' Colman insisted.

'The police . . . yes, of course. I suppose they'll have to be called now.'

'It's the second murder in two days. Of course we've got to bloody call them!' Anthony's patience was running out, and he got to his feet as Browning continued to dither. 'All right, then, I'll do it.' He turned to the Colonel. 'Someone will have to take charge until they get here, and you're the obvious choice. Can you gather everyone together and keep an eye on them, and make sure that no one goes near the Reverend's body?'

'Yes, of course. Whatever needs to be done. I'll send for some of the boys and we'll take care of it.'

'Thank you.' Anthony took Browning to one side. 'Is this exactly how you found him? Was there anyone else about?'

The manager shook his head, and it seemed to Elva that

he had suddenly become a very old man. 'I was about to clear those things away when the telephone rang at reception and I had to go and answer it,' he explained. 'I was only gone a few minutes. When I came back, this is what I found.'

'Where was the candlestick?'

'Lying next to him.'

'So why did you pick it up?'

Browning took a moment to answer. 'Because I knew it was my fault and I felt terrible about it. If I'd returned it to the dining room earlier, as I promised you I would, this might never have happened.' The same uncharitable thought had crossed Elva's mind, but still she felt sorry for him. 'If I'm honest, I panicked. When you came downstairs, I was wondering if I had time to put the candlestick back. It was a stupid idea, I know, and I probably wouldn't have done it, but after the trouble with the rope this morning I was worried about getting the blame.'

Anthony patted him on the shoulder. 'I know how you feel. I wish we'd never put them there. Go and look after Mrs Grayson. You both look like you could do with a brandy. I'll call the police.'

'But Miss Silver . . .'

'Yes, of course. I'll find out if they've made any progress.'

'I suppose the two deaths *are* connected?' Elva said as she and Anthony went to reception to use the telephone.

'It's one hell of a coincidence if they're not. Teal hints that he knows who the murderer is, and less than an hour later, he's hit over the head just like she was. God, Elva, I could kick myself. It's the first rule of detective fiction – never delay questioning a suspect, because they're bound to be bumped off before you get to them. Why wasn't I firmer with him in the vestry?'

'Because this isn't your responsibility,' Elva reminded him. Gently, she touched his arm, concerned now by how involved they had become. 'We're *not* the detectives here, Anthony. This is much too serious for us. Just telephone the police and hand the whole mess over to people who know what they're doing.'

To her relief, he made the call without any argument. 'Police please.' There was a brief pause while he was put through. 'Yes, hello. My name is Anthony Pratt and I'm telephoning from the Tudor Close Hotel. I want to report another murder. Yes, I did say another one, and I have a strong suspicion that the two deaths are connected.' She listened while he responded to questions, giving a brief account of what had happened the day before. 'Yes, that's what I said. Ethel Silver, spelt like the colour.' He rolled his eyes, impatient at having to repeat himself. 'Today's victim? His name is Reverend Teal, and he's the vicar of St Margaret's, Rottingdean. What? Well, yes, I suppose it *is* also spelt like the colour. No, of course that's not the connection. He was hit over the head like Miss Silver, but with a candlestick. Sorry, I didn't catch that. Where? Oh, in the hall, by the Christmas tree.' There was a long pause as the voice at the other end had his say. 'Hang on a minute,' Anthony said indignantly, 'I'm *deadly* serious. We've had two murders in two days here and we need you to send somebody . . .'

He jiggled the receiver rest and stared at Elva in disbelief. 'He's hung up on me. The bloody man's just put the phone down. Threatened me with wasting police time and told me to stay off the Christmas spirits.'

Under any other circumstances, Elva would have found his indignation funny. 'It did sound quite creative,' she said tactfully, 'but you'll have to try again. Unless you want me to have a go?'

He slid the phone across the desk a little huffily. 'Be my guest.'

Elva dialled again and tried a more direct approach. 'Hello, I'm speaking from Tudor Close in Rottingdean. We need urgent help. One of our guests has been killed.'

She listened for a moment, then said: 'Yes, that was my husband. No, it wasn't very clear and I'm sorry if he confused you – it's probably the shock.' She felt Anthony's glare and avoided his eye, keen to make her point now that she had the policeman's attention. 'He wasn't making anything up, though. The Reverend Teal was found dead about fifteen minutes ago, and we've really no idea what to do. Please come as soon as you can.' This time, she gave Anthony the thumbs up. 'Thank you, yes, I understand the snow will delay things, but we're very grateful. The army's looking after us, so we're in good hands until you get here, but it's all a bit frightening, especially after yesterday. Is there any news on Miss Silver's murder?' She listened intently, struggling to make sense of what the policeman was telling her. 'Perhaps you could talk to Inspector Clough,' she suggested. 'He took all the details.' Anthony was mouthing questions at her and she waved him away, trying to concentrate. 'He isn't? Really? What about Sergeant Devonshire? Oh, I see. Well, never mind. I mustn't hold you up, and the Reverend Teal is the priority at the moment. We'll see you as soon as possible, and no, we won't touch a thing.'

Bewildered, she put the receiver down and stared at Anthony. 'No wonder they thought you were barking mad,' she said. 'They know absolutely nothing about Miss Silver's murder, and they've never heard of Inspector Clough or Sergeant Devonshire. As far as the Sussex Police Force is concerned, they simply don't exist.'

5
AN 'ACCUSATION' IS MADE...

'I just don't understand it,' Anthony said for the umpteenth time, when he and Elva could finally escape to their room for a few minutes alone. Downstairs, an uneasy calm had descended and the Colonel had taken charge of the situation with a quiet authority that was appreciated by everyone. Guests had been offered the choice of waiting for the police alone in their bedrooms, or in one of the public areas under the polite but watchful eye of the Canadian infantry, and fear made them malleable; so far, no one had objected to a loss of freedom if it meant that they were safe. Unlike the day before, Mrs Grayson hadn't rallied from the shock sufficiently to serve the meal that was planned, but Browning pulled himself together, and – with the help of the younger, apparently unshockable kitchen staff – he managed to organise a hot and cold buffet for those with an appetite to eat it. The general consensus so far was that this would certainly be a Christmas to remember, but for all the wrong reasons.

Anthony sat down in one of the armchairs and stared into the empty grate. 'If Miss Silver's death was never reported, the only thing that makes sense is that those two men – let's call them Clough and Devonshire, just for the hell of it – actually killed her, then came back for some reason and found us there, so posed as policemen.'

'*Does* that make sense? It's quite some charade to make up on the spot. We'd have been *very* proud of that performance.'

'Perhaps it wasn't spontaneous. They might have had a contingency plan. Clough was carrying a warrant card, wasn't he?'

'But why would they want to kill Ethel Silver? And who are they?'

'And where does Teal's murder fit in? They're certainly not staying at the hotel – unless they're in number seven, of course...'

'Which is where the vicar was last night. I hadn't thought of that, but you're right – we've only got Browning's word for it that it's a Mrs Threadgold in there, whoever she is.' Elva considered the idea for a minute. 'Do you trust Browning?' she asked.

It was a question that Anthony had been wrestling with himself, unable to forget the image that had greeted him as he came down the stairs. 'Well, he was at Miss Silver's shop on the day she died, although he freely admitted as much, which he probably wouldn't have done if he'd had something to hide.'

'And he wasn't at the carol service to hear Teal's sermon, but he knew what had been said because some of the guests told him.'

'Why would he want to hurt either of them, though? I just don't see a motive.'

'So we're back to Rivers, then,' Elva said. 'We know something was going on between him and Miss Silver, and he certainly seemed either very angry or very frightened when Teal was speaking. He was holding on to the pew as if his life depended on it. Do you think he's strong enough to wield that candlestick? Nurse Blanchett implied he was at death's door.'

Anthony weighed it up. 'If he was desperate enough, I think he could do it. Or if his wife helped him.'

'They went straight upstairs to rest . . .'

'. . . but they could have come down again. They were certainly in the lounge by the time the body was found. And that's our problem, isn't it? Anyone could have come down from their room or in from outside and taken their chance in an empty hallway. It was an audacious thing to do, but it would only have taken seconds.'

'I suppose even Mrs Threadgold could have left her web

and scuttled back to it if she was lucky with the timing, and none of us would be any the wiser.'

Anthony sighed. 'All this speculation isn't getting us anywhere,' he said, standing up decisively. 'I think we should take a walk down to Miss Silver's.'

'What on earth for?'

'We might find a clue to what's going on.'

'Anthony, it's not safe. What if those men are still there? We've got away with it once and we shouldn't push our luck. Then there's the police – we don't want them to think we've done a runner if we're missing when they arrive. How will that look?'

'The police won't be here for ages. The roads out of town might be all right, but the country lanes into the village will have to be cleared before they can get anywhere near the place.' He went to the anteroom to fetch their coats and scarves. 'Please, Elva. If they did kill her, I can't bear the thought of her still lying there, all alone. That's not right. The police need to start an investigation for real, and we might be able to speed that along if we have a bit more information.'

Reluctantly, she agreed. 'All right, but we'll have to think of something to tell the Colonel. He's supposed to be keeping an eye on everyone, and that includes us.'

'We'll just say we're going to the car for something. He trusts us, so I don't think he'll insist on an escort.'

Anthony was right, and from the garages they slipped easily out into Dean Court Road and on to the Green, where children were skating gleefully on the frozen pond. The village looked splendid in the pale winter sun, and the snow had brought a rare harmony to the jumble of architectural styles and periods that usually distinguished the high street. Only the tiny sweet shop seemed immune now to the magic of the season: its blinds remained firmly pulled down, giving the whole building a sad, abandoned look. Perhaps it was Anthony's imagination, but even the painted sign above the door seemed to shine less brightly than it had the day before.

Without any great hope, he tried the front door, but it was firmly locked. 'You were right,' he said with a sigh. 'I don't know what I thought we were going to learn by coming here. We'll have a quick look round the back and then I'll admit defeat.' Elva humoured him by leading the way down a small passage that ran between two terraces, and they counted the houses back to Miss Silver's yard. 'Well, someone's definitely been here,' Anthony said, looking over the fence at the footprints in the snow. 'Probably our make-believe policemen.' The gate opened readily enough, but the back door was locked, as he had found it on Christmas Eve, and the tabby cat sat plaintively on the step, waiting in vain to be let in. Anthony bent down to stroke him, more saddened by this small casualty of the murder than he would have cared to admit, and the cat rubbed hopefully around his legs.

'We could ask the neighbour to put something down for him,' Elva suggested. 'He should be by a warm fire in this weather.'

'Yes, he should.' Anthony looked up at the silent house, frustrated at learning so little. Impulsively, he walked over to the coal bunker in the corner of the yard and picked up a shovel that lay covered in snow, then turned back to the window, but Elva put a hand on his arm. 'You're not seriously going to break in, are you?'

'Why not?'

'Because it's against the law. Because we don't know who's in there. Because you're accident-prone and you're bound to cut yourself. Because it's too late now to help her. How many more reasons do you want?' Her final point hit home, and he let her take the shovel from his hand. 'When the police get to Tudor Close, we'll talk to them properly and make them take us seriously, then *they* can come and look for Miss Silver. All right?'

Anthony nodded. 'If the bastards haven't disposed of her somewhere else.'

'Either way, there's no point in getting ourselves charged with breaking and entering. And perhaps Mrs Grayson will take the cat? We should go back to the hotel now, and I'll speak to her about it.'

'Let's at least go to the end of the road and have a look at the beach first. I'm not in a hurry to sit and wait with our fellow guests, are you? Not when any one of them could be a murderer.' He smiled, and added with a touch of wistfulness in his voice, 'Anyway, we promised ourselves a walk by the sea on Christmas Day.'

They carried on down the high street, across the main road and past the White Horse Hotel, a traditional seaside inn whose pale walls, modern design and open setting couldn't have contrasted more starkly with Tudor Close. Through the windows, Anthony could see Christmas lunch in full swing, untarnished by murder or suspicion, and suddenly he longed for the hotel's ordinary simplicity. He took Elva's hand and they walked down the curve of the steps to the shingle below. The crumbling chalk cliffs changed so quickly here, and already he could see places where familiar pathways or outcrops had been swallowed up by the sea since their last visit, but that wasn't as big a shock to him as the rolls of barbed wire that lined the beach, black and tangled and spiked, a sinister smudge of charcoal stretching away into the distance. Stupid of him, really, to think that this view would remain unchanged, but still it lowered his spirits. There had always been such a feeling of glamour about Rottingdean beach, in spite of the fierce winds that blew and the pungent line of seaweed that caught your ankles as you stepped out to swim. The white cliffs had dazzled in the sunlight, the sea always felt fresher and more exhilarating than anywhere else – but not today.

'It will all come back one day, won't it?' Elva said, as if following his thoughts, and he heard the break in her voice. 'Some sort of normal, I mean. Some sort of life.'

He pulled her close and kissed her. 'Of course it will. We have to keep believing that. Anything else is unthinkable.'

They watched the sea for a while, then, when they could stand the cold no longer, turned for home. 'Perhaps we should try and have a conversation with the Riverses this afternoon,' Elva suggested. 'We might learn something that will throw a bit of light on everything.' She stopped and glanced back, realising that she was talking to herself.

'Look at that.' Anthony pointed across the road to Miss Silver's upstairs window, where the tabby cat was now sitting on the windowsill, diligently licking his paw.

'Thank goodness!' Elva said. 'I hated the idea of him being out in the snow all night.'

'Yes, but how did he get in? The windows and doors are all shut and there's no cat-flap – and I doubt very much that he's got a key.'

'Oh, I see what you mean. Well, perhaps the neighbour . . .'

But Anthony didn't wait to hear the rest of the sentence. He hurried down the passage before Elva could stop him, and opened Miss Silver's gate. 'Someone's definitely in there,' he said, when she caught up with him. 'That shovel's not where you left it. It looks like whoever it is has fetched some coal.'

'We should call the police again.'

'What good would that do? It's not as if they're just round the corner. And anyway,' he added, still smarting from his telephone call, 'who's to say they'll even take us seriously? No, it's time for something a little more direct.' He picked up the shovel, but found that he didn't need it: this time, the back door opened as soon as he turned the handle. 'Wait here,' he whispered, ignoring Elva's attempts to hold him back.

'Not bloody likely,' she said, obviously furious with him. 'If you won't listen to reason, I don't see why I should.'

Except for the cold, empty grate, everything in the parlour looked exactly the same as it had the night before, but this time there was a faint smell of cooking on the air. Anthony picked up a fire poker and handed it to Elva, then armed himself with one of the sharper-looking knives from the kitchen drawer before tiptoeing out into the corridor. Gently, he opened the door to the storeroom and flicked on the light switch, experiencing an uncomfortable sense of déjà vu, but Miss Silver's body was gone, and the only sign of what had happened to her was a dark stain on the floor where someone had tried to remove the blood. He switched off the light again and checked that the shop was empty, then turned towards the stairs.

They were barely halfway up when one of the steps creaked loudly enough to wake the dead. Anthony paused and put a finger to his lips, hoping to have got away with it, but there was an answering sound from the room at the end of the landing – a dull thud, as if something had been pushed against the door, followed by the shuffle of footsteps.

He climbed the remaining stairs, and checked that the other two rooms were unoccupied. 'What are we going to do now?' Elva whispered, and he smiled reassuringly at her, reluctant to admit that he had absolutely no idea. Heartily wishing that he hadn't been quite so reckless, he put forward the best plan he could think of.

'Open the door and see what happens? Looking on the bright side, if they're hiding in there, maybe they're more frightened of us than we are of them.'

Before he could lose courage, he gave the door a hefty shove. The chair that had been pushed up against it slid away easily, leaving enough room for him to step inside. An elderly woman was cowering pitifully by the side of a single bed, shaking with fear, her arms covering her head in anticipation of a blow. As he moved towards her, she began to whimper like a cornered animal, and just for a second Anthony felt the same sense of anger and helplessness that was all too familiar to him from his nights on fire-watching duty in the raids over Birmingham. He hated to see people vulnerable and frightened, and his heart went out to the woman, even before he recognised her.

It was Ethel Silver.

'Anthony, what's going on? Who is it?' Elva tailed off as she joined him by the bed, and he saw his own bewilderment reflected back in her face. 'What on earth? But it can't be . . .'

At the sound of a woman's voice, Miss Silver lifted her head. 'Mrs Pratt, thank God. I heard you on the stairs and I thought he'd come for me.' She began to cry with relief and

Elva went to comfort her, helping her gently to her feet. 'It's all got out of hand,' she sobbed, her words barely discernible in her distress. 'None of this was supposed to happen, and now poor Christopher's dead and it's all our fault.'

'Do you mean the Reverend Teal?' Anthony asked, realising that they had never known his first name.

Miss Silver nodded. 'I never dreamt he'd be in danger like that. I couldn't believe it when Dorothy telephoned to warn me. She thinks that none of us are safe now, and she's right. I really don't know what to do.'

'But we thought you were already dead,' Anthony said, fishing a handkerchief out of his pocket and passing it to her. 'We thought you'd been murdered. I saw the walking stick covered in blood and your head . . .' Confused, he looked at her face but could see no sign of an injury. 'What's all this about?' he asked.

She began to cry again. 'God forgive us, but we just wanted to make Charles Rivers pay for what he did. I *swear* we didn't mean for anybody else to get hurt.'

'You'd better tell us everything, right from the beginning,' Elva said. 'Let's go downstairs and I'll make some tea. We could all do with something for the shock.'

They settled in the parlour and Elva fussed around, boiling a kettle and gathering cups until Miss Silver seemed calmer. 'Tell us what's going on,' Anthony said encouragingly, when she was settled with some hot, sweet tea and a medicinal sherry. 'Take your time, and we'll do what we can to help.'

'Well, it all started when the Riverses booked for Christmas and asked for the rooms from their old house. None of us could believe that they'd show their faces here again, not after what happened.' Anthony was dying to ask what that was, but he didn't want to interrupt her now that she'd started so he let her tell the story in her own way. 'We were horrified at first, but then we started to see it as a second chance. We let him get away with it last time because it was for the best, but now it was time to get justice.'

'Who's "we"?' Elva asked.

'Dorothy, Reginald and me.'

'All the people who'd worked for him.'

'That's right. And Christopher, too, of course. He helped us, just like he did fifteen years ago, and now he's paid dearly for it.'

Anthony wondered what that help consisted of. 'No wonder your sister didn't seem very upset by your death,' Elva said. 'I thought you just didn't get on.'

'No, nothing like that. Dorothy and me have always been close.'

'Was it her we saw leaving as we arrived?' Anthony asked.

'Yes, with George, her husband. They helped me set it all up, but you were earlier than we thought you'd be in that snow. George dropped Dorothy off at the Tudor then came straight back here with a friend of his who owed him a favour – we couldn't risk you calling the real police, obviously, so he didn't hang about.' She got up and fished in a drawer. 'Thank goodness you didn't look too closely at the warrant card. You might have recognised it.'

Anthony took it from her. 'It's the one from our old prop box,' he said. 'I wondered where it went.' He looked sheepishly at Elva, suddenly feeling very stupid at how easily he'd been fooled. 'You were taking quite a risk, relying on the fact that I wouldn't examine the body.'

'Not really. If you'd seen through it, we'd have just laughed it off as a joke, in keeping with the spirit of the weekend. You know how much I always loved the murder-mystery games you organised – we spoke about that on the telephone recently, Mrs Pratt – so I think you'd have believed me. Anyway, it was worth the gamble.'

'But why fake your own death?' Elva asked. 'What were you hoping to achieve?'

Miss Silver looked at each of them in turn, and smiled a

little sadly. 'It was you who gave us the idea, really. Christmas 1935 at Tudor Close – do you remember the murder mystery you did that year? It was one of your best. "The Conscience of the King", you called it – a play within a play, just like in *Hamlet*, and your characters told a story that was designed to flush out a real killer. Well, that's what we were trying to do.' She was right, Anthony thought: it was a scenario that they had been particularly proud of, and he remembered how well it had gone down and how enthusiastically everyone had taken part, especially Ethel Silver. 'Reginald suggested it,' she continued. 'He said he could easily persuade the owner of the hotel to invite you to stage another Christmas murder mystery, and we could use that somehow to frighten Rivers and incriminate him, to make you suspicious of him in the hope that he might finally be punished for what he did.'

'By framing him for something he *didn't* do?' Elva said. 'For a murder that didn't even happen?'

'We needed something that would shock you, something that you'd both care about, and I flattered myself that it would matter to you if I died. Anyway, you always said how important it was to start the game with a good body.' The joke fell flat, and Miss Silver looked from one of them to the other, challenging them to argue. 'It worked, though, didn't it? You took the bait. Dorothy said you'd been asking Reg about Rivers. You began to suspect that he'd killed me to cover up something he did in the past, and you wanted to know what that was. I think you'd have got to the truth, too.'

'But what was worth going to all that trouble for?' Elva demanded, conscious that her indignation stemmed at least in part from the knowledge that Miss Silver had a point. 'Why couldn't you just tell someone what you knew at the time?'

She hesitated. 'We had our reasons. We wanted justice – for Lily, of course, and for her sister – but we had no proof and no one would have believed us. Rivers had to be shamed or tricked into giving himself away.'

'"Time for you to make amends", Anthony quoted. 'We were always meant to get his Christmas card, I suppose? It wasn't a mistake that we ended up with that box of cigars.'

She shook her head. 'No, there was no mix-up, and it *is* time. It became even more urgent when we found out how ill he is. The thought of his dying without answering for any of it sickens me. He needs to be judged, in *this* life as well as in the next, just like Christopher said in his sermon.'

'Surely you weren't there?'

'No, but I knew what he was going to say. It was all part of the plan.'

'You're saying that this weekend was just one big murder-mystery game, and you used us to pull it off?' Anthony was becoming increasingly resentful of the way in which he and Elva had been manipulated, and there was an edge to his voice. 'Someone's been killed, and we're part of it?'

She looked at him, and there was a sadness in her eyes that made him want to retract the words. 'Yes, we probably did use you, but it certainly wasn't a game. If you'd been there while Rivers destroyed those children, if you'd seen what we saw, you'd understand.'

'Then tell us,' Elva said quietly. 'Help us to understand.'

Miss Silver fiddled nervously with the buttons on her cardigan, then took a sip of sherry for courage. 'Well, Dorothy and Reg worked for them for a few years before I joined them,' she began. 'The girls' old governess had left and Dorothy gave me the tip-off. Rivers refused to send them to school, you see. He said he wanted the best for those children and I suppose I was flattered by that when I got the job, especially with him being an academic man – he obviously valued what I could teach them. But there was more to it, I soon came to see that. Charles Rivers is the sort of man who isn't happy unless he's in control of everything around him – his staff, his wife, and especially his stepdaughters. He ruled that house with a rod of iron – literally, sometimes. Those girls used to shake at the sound of his voice.'

'How old were they then?' Elva asked.

'Lily was twelve and Rose seven. I tried to convince myself that there was nothing wrong with a bit of discipline, but it went against the grain to see children frightened like that. I suppose Dorothy and I were spoilt. We had a happy childhood, and we always knew we were safe and loved. It's what I would have given a child if I'd been lucky enough to have one, and it's what Dorothy's always given her two, but it wasn't my place to criticise or argue. Then things changed.'

'How?'

They waited for her to speak. When Anthony saw how difficult she was finding it, he almost didn't want to know the answer. 'I saw him coming out of the children's room one night,' she said eventually, her voice barely more than a whisper. 'He told me Lily was having a nightmare and he'd heard her crying, but I always listened out for the girls and I hadn't heard anything. Then I noticed Lily changing. She was such a lovely child when it was just the three of us – curious and outgoing and eager to learn – but she became withdrawn and quiet, even when Rivers was out of the house. She didn't concentrate on her work anymore, and she started to cling to me at bedtime, when she'd always been happy to go up early and read a book. She lost her appetite, too, and sometimes she'd say she was ill when I knew she wasn't. It took months, but eventually I got her to confide in me.' She was silent for a moment. 'Can you imagine how terrible it was to watch a child trying to find the words to describe what her stepfather was doing to her?'

It was a rhetorical question, but Anthony shook his head. Opposite him, he saw Elva close her eyes. 'What did you do?' he asked gently.

'I urged her to tell her mother. It seemed to me that Mrs Rivers was the only one who could put a stop to it, but I don't think Lily could bring herself to do it. She hanged herself the next day. I found her in her bedroom.' Miss Silver was staring resolutely ahead now, tears running silently down her face, and Anthony had no doubt that she was seeing again every horrific detail of the scene that had greeted her that day. 'I've never forgiven myself. *I* should have gone to Mrs Rivers, but I didn't think she'd believe me. I let Lily down.'

'Did your sister and Mr Browning know what was going on?'

'They knew what I suspected, but I'm not sure either of them believed me until it was too late. Reg was devastated when Lily died. He loved those girls with a kindness that they never got from their stepfather, and he was all for confronting the Riverses or going to the police, but we talked him out of it.'

'Why?'

She treated his naivety with something between scorn and pity. 'You think we'd have been believed? Our word against someone of Rivers's influence and standing in the village? We'd have been sacked on the spot, and it was no good relying on Mrs Rivers to help – she never said a word against her husband. No, we had to keep our jobs and make sure we were there to look out for Rose, because it was only a matter of time before Rivers started on her.'

'What happened to Rose?' Anthony asked, already fearing the answer.

Miss Silver looked down at the untouched cup of tea in her hands. 'It's funny. We've kept this secret for so many years that I don't know how to begin to tell it, but things came to a head during the Christmas at Tudor Close. It hadn't been a happy day. There was a lot of tension between the Riverses over the new house and they weren't really speaking, so it was awkward for all of us, as if one wrong word could light the blue touchpaper. I went to my room for a while, just to get away from it, then I heard a commotion in Rivers's study – it's part of room seven these days – so I went to see what was going on. Mrs Rivers was screaming hysterically and he was trying to calm her down. Then I saw Rose lying by the desk, so still and vulnerable. Rivers started to babble, saying that he'd pushed her and she'd hit her head on the corner of the desk, swearing that he never meant to kill her, while his wife stared at her daughter in disbelief. It was the only time I'd ever seen him lose his nerve, at a loss to know what to do.' She bowed her head. 'As shocked as I was, I enjoyed seeing him so frightened by the thought of a rope around his neck, the very thing that he'd driven Lily to do to herself. I'm not proud of that, but I can't deny it.'

'So the rope was there to taunt him this morning?'

'Yes. Reg put it there – and the note about the Mozart sonata.' Her face lit up for a moment. 'Lily was a wonderful pianist for her age, Mr Pratt – you'd have been impressed. That was her favourite piece. You could hear it wherever you were in the house.'

What an exceptional liar Browning was, Anthony thought, remembering how convincing he'd been when denying all knowledge of both incidents; in fact, the three conspirators had each put on a performance to be proud of. 'What happened next?' he asked, forcing his attention back to that fateful day.

'Reg had arrived by that time, and he was incandescent with rage. I thought he was going to hit Rivers, so I told the Professor to take his wife away and calm her down while I went to Rose. She was deathly pale, but there was a peace about her, too. God forgive me, but part of me was relieved that she couldn't be hurt anymore, that he couldn't defile her like he had her sister. I bent down to kiss her forehead, and that's when I realised that she was still breathing.'

'He *hadn't* killed her?'

'No, she was just unconscious. I told Reg, then I went to the door to let the Riverses know, but something stopped me – the conviction that Rose would be better off dead, I suppose, at least as far as her parents were concerned. If we told them the truth, she'd have to stay with them and everything would be ten times worse. She'd have died like her sister eventually, I honestly believe that. It galled me that Rivers wouldn't be punished for his cruelty, but the important thing was that Rose was safe. Everything else could wait, so we hatched a plan there and then.'

'A plan to do what?' Elva asked, but Anthony was one step ahead of her.

'To get Rose away from them, and make sure that Rivers believed he'd killed her. But how did you manage it?'

'I didn't hold out much hope, but in the end he made it easy. He begged us to keep quiet about what had happened, and offered us a ludicrous amount of money if we'd help him cover it up. So we accepted.'

'And you bought your shop with it?' Anthony guessed.

Miss Silver looked offended. 'I did no such thing. I had my own savings for that. No, I put it in trust for Rose. So did Reg. We never touched a penny of his filthy money.'

'Of course not,' Elva said, frowning at Anthony's lack of tact. 'What happened next?'

'Reg told the Riverses to go upstairs while we took care of everything, and I fetched Dorothy to let her know what was happening. Rose had come round by then, and I was terrified that her parents – or at least her mother – would want to see her again to say goodbye, but they didn't. That's how little they cared for her. It was out of sight, out of mind, and that made me even more certain that we were doing the right thing.'

'But where could you take her? None of you could look after her.'

'That's where Christopher came in. We knew we could trust him, and he didn't let us down.' There was a catch in her voice as she continued. 'He was a good man, and if I'd known what would happen all these years later, I'd never have involved him, but he was in touch with lots of organisations that looked after orphaned children, and he made all the arrangements. Dorothy took Rose to him that night, as soon as we'd made sure she was all right. There was a secret passage that ran from the study to the kitchen and then on to the church, and she used that. It's left over from the old smuggling days and Rose thought it was a great adventure.' She looked at them defiantly, as if expecting to have to defend herself. 'They'd already started, you know, the night-time visits. Rose told me that years later, so I've never regretted what we did. She went on to have a good life, with adoptive parents who love her and a family of her own now.'

'And the Riverses never suspected what you'd done?'

'Never. The next morning, we showed Rivers a patch of loose soil at the foot of the stairs to the passageway. To this day, he thinks his stepdaughter's buried there. They left the village soon afterwards and started a new life where nobody knew them.'

'So that's why he's so desperate to get into his old rooms.'

Miss Silver nodded. 'The passage is closed up now because it was dangerous, but the staircase is still there, and a cellar. As long as Reg was at Tudor Close to keep an eye, I suppose Rivers thought he was safe, but with the army about to commandeer the whole building, he'll be terrified of what they might find.'

'Except there's nothing *to* find,' Anthony said, enjoying the irony.

'But Rose *is* in there, isn't she?' Elva argued, and he looked at her in surprise. 'Just not in the way that Rivers thinks. Mrs Threadgold *is* Rose, isn't she?'

'She calls herself Elizabeth these days, but yes. When she heard her stepfather was dying, she wanted to confront him before it was too late. I was all for it, but now I'm terrified for her. She's not safe here. We've seen what Rivers is capable of, and now Christopher's dead. Who's to say what he'll do next?'

The sound of the telephone cut through the silence, ringing twice, stopping, then ringing again. 'That's Dorothy,' Miss Silver said, getting up to answer it. 'We have a signal so I always know it's her.' She went through to the shop and returned moments later, flushed and upset.

'What's happened?' Elva asked.

'It's Reginald. Dorothy says the police have just arrested him for Christopher's murder.' She looked pleadingly at them. 'We've got to do something. Please help us.'

Elva got up to comfort her, giving Anthony time to think. 'You've been right all along,' he said after a moment, squeezing Miss Silver's hand. 'We need Rivers to give *himself* away. It'll mean staging another performance, but I think I've got an idea.'

6
MRS THREADGOLD SHOWS HER CARDS

The sombre sight of a police ambulance greeted Anthony and Elva as they returned to Tudor Close. It was parked discreetly beside the row of garages, and Elva tried and failed to imagine something less in keeping with the spirit of Christmas Day.

'At least we can be sure it's a real murder this time,' Anthony said, with a heavy dose of irony. 'You know where you are with a mortuary van.'

It might not have been the most appropriate comment, but Elva understood exactly how he felt. She was still grappling with the twists and turns that the weekend had taken, with the deeply affecting emotions that Miss Silver's story had aroused in her and the bewildering mixture of reality and illusion that made everything seem so surreal. 'I've been wondering how Miss Silver will manage her resurrection in the village,' she admitted. 'She's got a lot of explaining to do to anyone who was at the carol service this morning.'

'They'll probably declare her a modern-day saint,' Anthony said, 'especially if she can hold out till Easter.'

'And it's no more than she deserves. Whatever we think

of what's happening now, what they did all those years ago was incredibly brave.'

'But not without its consequences.'

His tone was suddenly more serious, and Elva followed his gaze to the shrouded figure being carried from the hotel on a stretcher. They stood aside to let the small party pass, and Anthony removed his hat. For Elva, the sadness of the scene only emphasised the gravity of what they were about to attempt, and she looked doubtfully at her husband. 'Do you think we can pull this off?' she asked.

'We have to if we're to get Browning off the hook and justice for Reverend Teal. We'll need Colonel Colman on side, though – that's our first priority. What we're asking Rose – sorry, Elizabeth – to do is quite risky, and we don't want any mistakes. We know all too well now what Rivers is capable of.'

'I wonder what she's like?'

'We'll soon find out. Let's just hope that her stepfather takes the bait.'

The Colonel met them in the entrance hall and raised a conspiratorial eyebrow. 'Did you have trouble finding it?'

'Finding what?'

'Whatever it was you went to the car for three hours ago.' He smiled but didn't pry any further, and Elva felt as if she were being reprimanded by a favourite uncle. 'You missed quite a lot while you were gone. The police have left for now but they want a statement from you both as soon as possible, and they've arrested Mr Browning for the Reverend Teal's murder.'

'So we heard,' Anthony said, and Colman looked puzzled. 'I'll explain how we know that in a minute, but why did they single out Browning?'

The Colonel shrugged. 'Everyone else had an alibi. Mrs Grayson was in the kitchen with her staff. The Riverses and Nurse Blanchett were in the lounge, and the other guests were either at the bar or already in the dining room. I was in the conservatory, talking to a couple who have a cousin in Canada and wondered if I knew her, and the officers I was meeting for lunch were in the billiard room. Only Browning was on his own, in the hall . . .'

'. . . with the candlestick, yes. I can see how it looks, but that isn't the whole story.'

Elva looked at her watch. 'You should tell the Colonel everything while I go upstairs,' she said. 'Miss Silver should have made her phone calls by now, and—'

'Miss Silver?' Colman interrupted. 'I thought Miss Silver was dead?'

Elva left Anthony to explain and hurried upstairs,

feeling curiously nervous about the woman she was shortly to meet. She glanced round to make sure that no one had followed her up, then knocked the agreed number of times at the door to number seven; it was answered immediately, and she was ushered inside to a spacious landing with bedrooms leading off it.

Elizabeth Threadgold was tall and attractive, with blonde hair and a pale face that echoed her mother's colouring. 'I'm sorry to be a stranger barging in on you,' Elva said, when she had introduced herself, 'but hopefully Miss Silver will have told you to expect me?'

'She did, but you really don't feel like a stranger. Ethel used to tell me about the weekends she spent with you and your husband. It was hard for me to believe that anyone could ever have fun in this place after the brief time I spent here as a child, but they were happy days for her, so I feel like I know you a little already. And please, call me Elizabeth.'

'You took your sister's middle name?'

'Yes, it seemed the least I could do. I survived our family and she didn't, so I wanted her to be remembered. And I loved her. Obviously I never knew any different, but I can't imagine having a kinder big sister. There isn't a day goes by when I don't wish that she were still here, now more than ever.'

She led the way downstairs, and Elva looked through open doorways at the sumptuous but somewhat impersonal accommodation, trying to imagine it as the family home it had once been. The house's original front door opened onto the courtyard gardens; earlier in the day, sunlight would have poured through the stained-glass panels to drench the hallway with a kaleidoscope of colour, but now there were only shadows. 'It must be hard to spend time here on your own,' she said. 'Too many memories, very few of them happy.'

'I was dreading it, but it's done me good, I think.'

'In what way?'

'I've had time to realise what a sham it is. Nothing's what it seems here, is it? It's all a façade, just like the Rivers family. The respectability, the values, the love, even the grief when Lily died – none of it goes beyond the surface. It's all about what people see, and what you can make them believe.' She smiled sadly, and just for a second Elva was allowed a glimpse of the lasting damage that Elizabeth's early life must have done, but the window was soon closed again. 'It should have been the perfect house, quite literally built for us, but we were so insular, so isolated that it allowed my parents to make their own rules. I understand that now, and once you see through something, it loses its power, don't you think? So it's helped, more than I ever thought possible. Still, I won't be sorry to leave.' She opened the door to a small sitting room and showed Elva inside. 'This is my stepfather's old study, the room where I'm supposed to have died. The trapdoor to the secret passage is over by the hearth.' Her composure was remarkable and Elva couldn't help but think that in this, at least, she was her mother's daughter; Elizabeth's coolness, though, seemed to stem less from detachment than from an inner strength and resilience. 'Now,' she said, 'talk me through this plan of yours.'

Elva did as she asked. 'Well, we're fairly sure he'll let himself into the suite from the hotel landing upstairs rather than the front door in the courtyard – it's much less conspicuous.'

'And you want me to stay out of the way until he's in the passage?'

'Yes, that's really important. We need to prove that he thinks you're down there, so don't confront him before he gets there.'

'And what do I do if he doesn't go to the study? What if he just looks round the rest of the suite?'

'Then you stay out of sight until he leaves, and if he rumbles you, there'll be plenty of us here to step in. The plan will have failed, but at least you'll be safe. We'll make sure of that.' Elva paused, remembering how young the woman was in spite of her self-assurance. 'Are you sure you want to do this?' she asked. 'Everyone will understand if it's just too difficult.'

Elizabeth smiled. 'You're very kind, but I've never been more sure of anything in my life. I've waited too many years to ask too many questions, and I won't give up now.'

'Right then, I'll be back soon with reinforcements. Bolt the door as soon as I've gone, and don't open it again unless you know it's me. Once we're in the suite with you, leave the bolts undone so that your stepfather can use the key he took from reception.'

Downstairs, the entrance hall was piled with suitcases and Anthony stood behind the desk. 'You'd make a very handsome concierge,' she said, giving him a kiss. 'Where are the Riverses?'

'She's gone to their room but he's still in the lounge, thank God. I thought for a minute we were going to lose them both. Everything all right upstairs?'

'Absolutely. She's a remarkable young woman, you know. I hope this works for her.'

'Stand by,' Anthony said, glancing over at the door. 'Here comes our cue.'

The door swung open and Elva recognised Inspector Clough – or George Grayson, as she now knew him to be – this time wearing a chauffeur's peaked cap and driving gloves, no doubt another product of Miss Silver's obliging prop store. He winked when he saw them, then bellowed at the top of his voice: 'Car for Mrs Threadgold.' The volume was far more than the space required, but he repeated it just for good measure and Elva had to stop herself from cheering when she saw Rivers standing in the lounge doorway, looking out at the new arrival. A woman appeared at the top of the stairs, dressed in the smart black coat that Elva had lent her for the charade, and made her way slowly down to reception, while Grayson loaded the suitcases into a car outside. She went over to the desk, and Rivers watched her like a hawk as she handed her key over and signed the piece of paper that Anthony offered her. Then, without a backward glance, Mrs Threadgold – better known as the Tudor's kitchen maid, Gladys – ostentatiously left the building.

'Stage one safely completed,' Anthony said. 'Now we'd better get upstairs and into position before Rivers tries his luck.'

Colman was already waiting on the landing with one of his men, and they made their way quickly to room seven.

'So far, so good,' Elva said to Elizabeth as she let them in. 'I'll do the introductions later. Let's get ourselves settled and keep our fingers crossed.'

They each found somewhere to hide in the rooms downstairs, making sure that Elizabeth had a clear enough view of the study to judge when it was safe to emerge. Ten minutes went by, then fifteen, and Elva was just beginning to give up hope when she heard the door close softly upstairs and footsteps creeping down to the ground floor. She longed to look, but knew she couldn't risk it; only when Elizabeth came quietly out from the dining room and nodded an affirmative could she be sure that their target was in sight.

The Riverses' daughter walked quietly across the hall to the study, and everyone else followed. The trapdoor by the hearth was already raised, and Elva watched as Elizabeth stood there, looking down. There were tears in her eyes now, and Elva wondered what she would say to open this most painful of conversations. When it came, the question was simple but deadly.

'Are you looking for me, Daddy?'

Perhaps it was Elva's imagination, but there was a haunting, childlike quality to the voice, and she wished fervently that she could see its effect on Rivers; he must be bewildered.

'It's me, Rose. Surely you recognise me?'

The response was muffled, but not enough to conceal the raw desperation in the words. 'You're not my daughter. You *can't* be . . .'

'Why? Because she's buried under that pile of earth? Nothing to mark her passing but an extra letter on a tombstone?' Elizabeth smiled as her stepfather walked into the first snare that she'd laid for him. 'You really should have checked I was dead. That was careless of you. Thank God someone else did.' Teasingly, she made to close the trapdoor, and Elva didn't need to see Rivers to know the panic he must be feeling; it was clearly written in the look of satisfaction on his stepdaughter's face. 'All right then, come back up and talk to me,' she said. 'I'm not a ghost, I promise. You can touch me if you like.'

The last comment was heavily loaded, and Anthony was obviously concerned. As they heard Rivers begin to climb the ladder, he signalled to Elizabeth to step back from the opening, encouraging her to keep her distance. When her stepfather emerged into the room, he looked first in surprise, then in growing anger at his reception committee. 'What the hell's going on?' he demanded. 'Who's responsible for this charade?'

He seemed more affronted by the fact that he'd been

tricked than by the trouble in which he found himself, and Elva wondered if this really was the first time in his whole life that someone had stood up to him. She looked in admiration at Elizabeth, wishing that circumstances had allowed her to get to know the girl better.

'Your stepdaughter needs some answers, sir,' Colman said, with disarming politeness. 'We're just here to make sure she gets them.'

'But first I'd like my mother to join us,' Elizabeth said. 'Where is she?'

'Leave her out of this,' Rivers insisted. 'I'm warning you...'

Colman moved towards him, but Elizabeth seemed immune to the threat. 'You don't want her caught up in it? How chivalrous, but *I* want to see her.' She stared at him, and some acknowledgement passed between them before Rivers looked away. He obviously didn't want his wife to hear what his stepdaughter was going to say to him, and as Elva wondered what it would be like for Celia Rivers to find out exactly what had been going on behind her back, she almost felt sorry for the woman. 'Will someone fetch her for me?' Elizabeth asked.

Colman nodded to his sergeant and the rest of them waited in silence. When Celia Rivers entered the room with Nurse Blanchett at her side, there could be no doubt that she recognised her daughter immediately. She stumbled and cried out, and, while the nurse helped her to a seat, Elva was struck by her response: there was no relief or sudden outpouring of love, no greeting of any sort after so long – just pure, naked fear.

'We were reminiscing about our first Christmas here,' Elizabeth said. 'I'm sure you remember it? It was fifteen years ago to the day, almost to the hour, that my stepfather killed me and had me buried in that passageway.' She paused and looked directly at her mother, and in that fraction of a second Elva guessed what she was about to say. 'Except that isn't quite what happened, is it? It was *you* who hit me that day, not him, and it wasn't an accident. You took me by the hair and slammed my head against the corner of his desk because you thought he loved me more than he loved you. You knew damned well what he was doing to me, what he'd done to Lily, and you were jealous of the attention. You blamed *us* for it, not him, and you took it out on me that Christmas.' The words poured out of her and she stopped to take a breath, then addressed Anthony and Elva. 'He lied to Ethel to protect my mother, just like she'd always lied to protect him. Yes, he abused us, but she turned a blind eye to it for years. They're as bad as each other.'

There was a stunned silence in the room, and it fell to Nurse Blanchett to break it. 'Is this true, Celia?'

'Of course it's not,' Rivers snapped, before his wife could speak. 'I pushed her, just as I said I did back then, but it was an accident, I swear.'

Elizabeth gave a bitter laugh. 'There you go again. Lies on top of lies. What's the plan? That you save her neck and die a hero? One noble act to clean up all the dirt? You weren't even in the room when it happened.' She jabbed a finger at her mother. '*She* was responsible for my so-called death, and for Lily's before that.'

'Are you saying that Lily's death wasn't suicide?' Anthony asked.

'No, just that she drove her to it.' Elizabeth sat down on the sofa next to Mrs Rivers, the parody of a daughter confiding in her mother. 'I know she came to you the day before she died, and I heard what you said to her. I didn't understand then, but I do now – I understood from the moment he started to do it to me. Do you have any idea how much courage it took for her to tell you? And all she wanted to hear was that you believed her, that you didn't blame her. She wanted you to take the fear away. Isn't that what mothers do?' Celia Rivers was staring down at her lap and Elva longed to get up and shake her, to force her to look at her daughter. 'I heard you slap Lily, then you accused her of lying,' Elizabeth said, and it was obviously an effort now to keep her voice even. 'You said our stepfather was a good man and she was evil for suggesting otherwise. *Evil?* She was fourteen years old, for God's sake. But you scolded her and you silenced her, and I remembered that when he started on me. It taught me that I didn't have a voice and I didn't have a friend. Whenever he hurt me, I thought it was my fault because of what you said to Lily. I tried to be good so he wouldn't notice me. I didn't want to be pretty or liked, all the things that a little girl should be allowed to be. I didn't want to feel special. And that's something my daughter will always feel, God help me, if it takes the last breath in my body.'

Finally, Rivers broke his silence. 'We have a granddaughter?'

She stared at him in disbelief, then threw back her head and laughed. 'You have *nothing*. You're not my family. My family are the people who saved me that night – your servants, who you treated like dirt. They found parents to care for me and they've looked out for me all my life – and I love them for it.' Her stepfather looked as if he were about to argue, but she cut him off. 'Dorothy, who carried me along that passage and showed me more tenderness in ten minutes than you did in years. I should have been terrified, but somehow I knew I was finally safe. And Ethel and Mr Browning, who always did their best to shield me from you, who gave me money – the money you paid them to keep quiet – to make sure I had a decent start in life and wouldn't *ever* need to be dependent on a man like you. And the Reverend Teal . . .' Her voice faltered at the mention of his name, and she bowed her head. 'The man you killed, because you thought he was going to expose what you did.'

'I didn't kill him,' Rivers insisted. 'Browning did it. The police have him in custody.'

'How very convenient,' Anthony said sarcastically, 'but perhaps you're telling the truth.' Everyone looked at him in surprise, Elva included. 'Not about Mr Browning – he certainly didn't do it – but perhaps you didn't, either. Nurse Blanchett, did Professor Rivers leave the lounge at all in the fifteen minutes before the Reverend's body was found?' Reluctantly, she shook her head. 'And what about Mrs Rivers? Was she there all the time?'

There was a silence as the nurse stared at Celia Rivers, and her answer was obvious even before she spoke. 'You went up to the room,' she said, as if she didn't want to believe her own testimony. 'You were gone for about five minutes, perhaps a little longer. It crossed my mind at the time, but I didn't say anything because I never thought you'd be capable of something like this.'

'And I'm not!' Celia looked desperately at her husband. 'Tell them, Charles. It was you, not me.'

From the moment she'd first set eyes on her in reception, Elva had found Mrs Rivers's cool detachment from the world unnerving; by contrast, its sudden collapse was contemptible to watch, and it highlighted more than anything the differences between mother and daughter – never in a million years could Elva imagine Elizabeth crumbling in this way. Now, it seemed as if the understanding between husband and wife, whatever that had been, was finally at an end. 'Emily, you can't believe I'd do this,' Mrs Rivers said, turning elsewhere for support as the Professor remained stubbornly silent. 'What about our plans?' She reached out to take her friend's hand, but the nurse recoiled as if she'd been scalded. 'He forced me, I swear. I never wanted to do it.'

'I don't believe you, Celia. He's a lot of things, but I never once saw him hurt you or threaten you. And what about everything else? They were your *children*, for God's sake. How could you let him do that?'

She got up and left the room without another word.

Colonel Colman stepped forward, obviously having heard enough to convince him that the truth of the Reverend's murder was a matter to be decided between the police and the Riverses. 'I need you to come with me, sir, while we wait for the police,' he said, 'both you and your wife.' He took the professor's arm and directed the sergeant towards Mrs Rivers. Much to Elva's surprise, they both allowed themselves to be led meekly out of the study towards the stairs.

'Wait a minute,' Elizabeth said, standing in her mother's path. 'Why did you let it happen? I still don't understand. Was it just because you couldn't bear the shame of it all coming out? Or did you really love him so much more than you loved us?' But Celia Rivers wouldn't even meet her eye. She was led away and Elizabeth was left to stare after her, having the promise of some sort of justice, but still without the answers she needed to make sense of her past. All Elva could hope was that – having had the strength to confront her parents – she could now look to the future and have the life she deserved.

As soon as the Riverses had left the suite, Dorothy Grayson appeared on the stairs, followed by her sister. 'I had to come,' Ethel said, clasping their hands. 'I hope you don't mind. I know we agreed I'd wait at the shop, but I couldn't rest until I knew it had all gone to plan and everyone was safe.'

'Of course we don't mind,' Elva said. 'You should be here. There's a young lady over there who'll be very pleased to see you.' She looked across to where Dorothy was hugging Elizabeth, both of them crying with relief. 'She was astonishingly brave today, but she needs you more than ever now. We'll give you some privacy.'

'And will they let Reg go?' Ethel asked, catching her arm.

'Absolutely,' Anthony promised. 'It might take a bit of time to unravel everything, but I'd put money on his being back for Boxing Day.'

Elva took his hand and they left the suite by the courtyard entrance, walking out into the snow. It was funny how different everything felt, she thought. When they had arrived on Christmas Eve, the darkness over Tudor Close had been oppressive and threatening, coloured by the shock of the murder they thought they had uncovered; tonight, in spite of the day's sadness and the very real violence, there was a peacefulness about the hotel, a sense that some things, at least, had been resolved. No doubt the feeling was entirely down to her imagination, fostered by relief and by the odd light here and there that – in Browning's absence – defied the blackout, but still she found it comforting.

'Is it really only twenty-four hours since we got here?' Anthony said, as they walked across to the porch. 'It's certainly been quite a Christmas.'

'It has, but I think I'm ready to leave it behind, aren't you?'

She looked at him, afraid that he might be disappointed, but he just smiled. 'You have no idea how much I was hoping you'd say that. If there's no more snow overnight, we can make an early start and be back in time to have our own Christmas at home.'

'That's music to my ears.'

Realising suddenly how hungry they were, they raided the buffet and retreated to their room. When they had eaten and packed, ready for the morning, they dozed by the fire for a while, glad to have nothing more to worry about than an early alarm call. Just after ten o'clock, they were woken by a discreet knock at the door and Anthony went to answer it.

'I hope I'm not disturbing you,' Browning said, as he was welcomed into the room, 'but I couldn't let the day end without thanking you both for what you've done. I don't mind admitting, I thought I'd had it for a while there. Ethel and the Colonel told me what you did, and I'm so grateful.'

'There's no need,' Elva said, giving him a hug. 'We're just pleased you're back safe and sound. How is Elizabeth?'

'Not bad at all, under the circumstances. Her husband's got a couple of days' leave – he's in the Air Force – so he's bringing little Millie over tomorrow. She's been staying with his parents but missing her mother, so it'll be nice for them to spend some of Christmas together, and we'll all be here to make sure they're well looked after.'

'Does Mr Threadgold know what she's been through?' Anthony asked.

'Oh yes, she told him right at the start and he's been very supportive.'

'So you'll all be having a proper family Christmas,' Elva said, and she was touched by how pleased he seemed at the description.

'Yes, I suppose we will – and you'll stay, won't you?'

There was an awkward pause, then Elva jumped in a little too enthusiastically. 'We'd love to,' she said, 'but we've got to leave first thing in the morning. Anthony has to work the next day and we don't know how the roads will be . . .'

'. . . and you've had more than enough of a Tudor Christmas for one year?' Browning smiled and waved away her apologies. 'I completely understand. I hope you'll come back, though. Perhaps when the war's over, if we all get through it in one piece?'

'If we can get through this weekend, we can get through anything,' Anthony said. 'Yes, of course we'll come back.'

7
AT A SPOT MARKED 'X'

When they arrived back at Stanley Road just after lunch, it was as if Christmas had never existed. 'It seemed sensible not to do ourselves up when we thought we wouldn't be at home,' Elva said, looking round the cheerless sitting room. 'And it's bloody freezing in here. I'm beginning to wish we'd stayed at the Tudor after all.'

'Half an hour and we'll have it ship-shape,' Anthony insisted, rubbing his arms to warm up. 'You start with the fire and I'll get everything out of the car.'

He brought the cases inside and unloaded their Christmas presents, still wrapped, onto the floor. 'They look a bit lost without a tree,' Elva said, 'but at least they're colourful.'

'Give me a minute, and I'll get us the next best thing.'

He opened the back door and went out into the garden, and she watched, laughing, as he gathered an armful of holly and spruce, getting the turn-ups of his trousers soaking wet in the snow on the lawn and bringing little trails of ice and water back into the house with him. 'You're completely mad but I love you,' she said, hugging him a little more tightly than usual. 'I'm glad to be home, aren't you? There were a couple of moments yesterday when I thought we might not make it.'

Dorothy had insisted on packing them off with a hamper of food to see them through the rest of the holiday, and Elva laid everything out on the dining-room table while Anthony opened the bottle of claret that Browning had given them as a thank you. 'This is good stuff,' he said, standing it to warm by the fire. 'All in all, I'd call that a damned fine Christmas spread.'

'And don't forget these.' Elva handed him the box of cigars. 'Perhaps you'll finally get to smoke one this evening.'

She lifted the lid and her drawing of the room plan at Tudor Close fell out onto the floor. Anthony pounced on it. 'There it is! I was worried we'd left it behind.' He propped it up on the piano with the Christmas cards. 'I had a few ideas coming along in the car ...'

Elva groaned. 'Haven't you had enough of murder mysteries for now?' She settled down on the sofa with the box of chocolate liqueurs that Miss Silver had given them. 'Go on then, but don't be surprised if I get through all of these before you've finished.'

Anthony grinned. 'Listen carefully and tell me what you think,' he said enthusiastically. 'A body has been found at the foot of the cellar stairs at a spot marked "X" . . .'

AUTHOR'S NOTE

Like thousands of people, I've loved *Cluedo* since I was a child. It was the board game of choice in my family, and I still have the 1970s version that I played then, complete with my mum and dad's handwriting on the old detective notes, and my own workings-out, which seem to be nothing but question marks. I'm not much better at it today, but its reliance on luck and logic (not unlike writing a detective novel) still make it a joy to play.

I also loved *Cluedo* because it was a game with a narrative – a narrative that was different every time, and one that the players had a hand in inventing. Long before I read Josephine Tey or Agatha Christie, it was *Cluedo* that gave me a love of crime fiction, and in particular of the classic English detective story and its obsession for knowing (or concealing) who did what, where and how.

To my shame, though, it had never occurred to me to wonder who I had to thank for all those hours of pleasure until I read an article somewhere about Anthony Pratt and his wife Elva, who created *Cluedo* together in 1943. Originally subtitled 'Murder at Tudor Close', the game took its setting from the famous hotel in Rottingdean that the couple had visited before the war, during Anthony's days as a musician; its playful murder premise was inspired by his love of detective novels and fascination with true crime, and by the country-house murder-mystery games that he and Elva used to take part in all around the country. They developed the game on a dining room table in Birmingham as an antidote to the worries and boredom of war, and – when wartime shortages were finally over – it was released by Waddingtons in December 1949.

There were more suspects in Anthony and Elva's original version: Mr Brown, Mr Gold, Miss Grey and Mrs Silver were eventually cut, while Nurse White became Mrs White and Colonel Yellow was changed to Colonel Mustard to avoid any connotations of cowardice in the military. In the American version, called *Clue*, Reverend Green became Mr Green, as a member of the clergy couldn't possibly be associated with murder. The weapons, too, looked a little different in the early plans and included poison, a bomb, a syringe, a poker and a shillelagh (Irish walking stick).

The Pratts sold the rights in 1953, but – despite the many changes and reinventions that the game has undergone – *Cluedo* remains true to their original, brilliant vision. *The Christmas Clue* is a very belated thank you.

ACKNOWLEDGEMENTS

Writing *The Christmas Clue* was a joy from start to finish, and much of that has been due to the enthusiasm of everyone else who works to bring the book to life. My thanks go to:

Veronique Baxter, for loving the idea before I'd even finished the sentence and for making the whole thing possible, and her colleagues Sara Langham, Kara Abraham and all at David Higham Associates. Everyone at Faber, especially Lochlann Binney, Sophia Cerullo, Walter Donohue, Joanna Harwood, Louisa Joyner, Ruth O'Loughlin, Hannah Turner and Phoebe Williams; the imagination and care that you bring to every aspect of every book never ceases to amaze me. Hayley Shepherd, for eagle eyes and insightful suggestions, and Joe McLaren, for making the map a work of art in itself. Lindsay and Gill, for gamely accepting that a dinner invitation *always* involved a game of *Cluedo*. And to Mandy, for making each day special, in every room on the board.

It's been wonderful for me to be in touch with Marcia Lewis, Anthony and Elva Pratt's daughter, and I appreciate her good wishes for the book more than I can say.

Also by Nicola Upson

The Dead of Winter

December 1938, and storm clouds hover once again over Europe. Josephine Tey and Archie Penrose gather with friends for a Cornish Christmas, but two strange and brutal deaths on St Michael's Mount – and the unexpected arrival of a world famous film star, in need of sanctuary – interrupt the festivities. Cut off by the sea and a relentless blizzard, the hunt for a murderer begins.

Pivoting on a real moment in history, *The Dead of Winter* draws on all the much-loved conventions of the Golden Age Christmas mystery, whilst giving them a thrilling contemporary twist.

'Unforgettable . . . not just for Christmas but for life.' *The Times*

'In a tightly structured plot, the feeling of menace and fear is kept at a high pitch by first-class writing.' *Daily Mail*

'Always a delight.' *Sunday Times*

faber

Also by Nicola Upson

An Expert in Murder

Death is not a rehearsal . . .

It's March 1934, and Golden Age crime writer Josephine Tey is travelling from Scotland to London to celebrate what should be the triumphant final week of her much-admired play, *Richard of Bordeaux*. However, a seemingly senseless murder puts her reputation, and even her life, under threat.

An Expert in Murder is both a tribute to one of the most enduringly popular writers of crime and an atmospheric detective novel in its own right.

'A wonderful period murder mystery [. . .] Fans of Tey herself and Agatha Christie will relish this both for its authenticity and its gripping plot.' *Evening Standard*

'A highly original and elegantly-written novel.' P. D. James

faber

Also by Nicola Upson

Shot With Crimson

I will never understand why murder is considered such a lowbrow speciality in Hollywood . . .

September, 1939, and the worries of war follow Josephine Tey to Hollywood, where a different sort of battle is raging on the set of Hitchcock's *Rebecca*.

Then a shocking act of violence reawakens the shadows of the past, with consequences on both sides of the Atlantic, and Josephine and DCI Archie Penrose find themselves on a trail leading back to the house that inspired a young Daphne du Maurier – a trail that echoes *Rebecca*'s timeless themes of obsession, jealousy and murder.

'An astonishingly complex mystery.' *The Times*

'Upson is chillingly effective at showing how good intentions may lead to evil consequences, especially when tainted with a dash of arrogance.' *The Spectator*

faber